STONECUTTER

STONECUTTER

LEANDER WATTS

Houghton Mifflin Company
Boston 2002

www.houghtonmifflinbooks.com

The text of this book is set in 13-point Lapidary

Library of Congress Cataloging-in-Publication Data
Watts, Leander.
Stonecutter / by Leander Watts.
p. cm.
Summary: In 1835 in rural New York State, apprentice stonecutter Albion Straight relates his experiences when he is hired by the strangely menacing John Good to carve a statue of his daughter.
ISBN 0-618-16474-X
[1. Apprentices—Fiction. 2. Stonecutters—Fiction. 3. Diaries—Fiction. 4. New York (State) — History—1775–1865—Fiction.] I. Title.
PZ7.W339 St 2002
[Fic] — dc21
2002000409

Manufactured in the United States of America

QUM 10 9 8 7 6 5 4 3 2 1

September 2

The comet appeared again, with a brilliant head and fiery white beard. I stood a long while in the Proctors' hayfield, watching the bright ball of skyfire. All around it, the stars were blotted out by its strange milky glow.

Little Watty was with me. He ate an apple down to the seeds, as tho this were more important than a sign in the heavens. Then he listened to the sky and pointed up at the comet.

"It hisses like Mamma's teakettle."

In Little Watty the powers of fancy far outweigh both sense and reason. He's only eleven years old, but there are times when it seems the three years between us is a vast distance. I'm not yet a man but certainly he is still a boy.

I heard nothing but a hooty owl, far-off in the woods, preaching to the darkness.

Earlier today, Mr. Bonness said that the comet will ride in the sky for the next seven nights. He consulted his almanack and found it in the chart of celestial events there. "Comet Halley, to appear in the western sky first week in

September 1835." He explained to me that this comet had visited our sphere twice before, in 1759 and 1682.

But the Reverend Mr. Yates had said at meeting yesterday that this was no mere mathematical repetition but a sign and a wonder, foretelling dire times.

The reverend led us in singing "The Trumpet," and the words were as awesome to my ears as if Gabriel himself were blowing in the heavens.

He comes, He comes, the trumpets sound
And loudly rends the vast profound.
Earth, sea and skies astonished shake
to judgment come, ye dead awake.

I had carved those very words on a gravestone only six months before, one of the first inscriptions Mr. Bonness allowed me to do with no assistance. It was a goodly-sized stone, almost as tall as I. He made the signs — an angel with trumpet as long as a musket — and I carved the saying. But singing those words with a score of good Christian folks and then seeing the comet, I was struck by a hammerblow of amaze.

It lit the sky better than a pitch-pine torch or a hundred tallow candles. It burned there, out to the west over the Genesee, like a bright knifewound in the black flesh of the sky. And I was afraid.

What if Mr. Yates is correct, and we are living in the end times? Mr. Bonness says this is foolishness. "Comets come and comets flee. Droughts one year and floods the next." Tho he carves angels and death's heads, weeping willows and hourglasses with wings as symbols for the passage of time, Mr. Bonness does not fear the future.

He paged back through his pile of almanacks and found that a rain of shooting stars had lit the sky in the season of my birth. "And surely, Albion, you'll not tell me that your borning was heralded by omens in the sky." He never mocks the Reverend Yates, but I suspect there's little warmth of feeling between the two men. They must work together: a minister of God and the gravestone cutter are often joined by a day's sad labor. But Mr. Bonness seldom attends meeting and never to my knowledge reads of the Bible. "Wonders will appear," he told me. "This year, and next and next. And all the years that you'll live. On the day of Little Watty's birth, a two-headed calf was born only a league hence. But that cast neither a blessing nor a curse on him."

I did not disagree. But Watty Bonness is a strange

child, listening to what I can never hear. He told me not long after I began as his father's apprentice that he can talk to the crows. This, I doubt extremely. But still he knows certain things that no other boy should know.

Mr. Bonness poked his finger hard on the almanack's astronomical chart. "The sky is as a vast and beautiful clockwork. Men who've studied natural philosophy can determine its phases and seasons. This comet is no divine sign."

I nodded and got busy again with chisel and hammer. I have another day's work 'til I'm done with the watering trough for Martin Silver. But I could not keep from thinking on the comet and on the words that Watty said last night when we were looking up at the sky. "I see the comet and the comet sees me."

September 3

I commence again, a better beginning to this journal. Yesterday's words came quickly. I find the quill flies over the pages. But I think it more fitting to announce myself proper and establish the purpose of this writing.

As the words of the first entry are fixed and well-dry, I'll not rub them away. But I desire to step back and lay a foundation before the house — my life so far — is built up in words.

So here again begins the journal of Albion Straight. My mother passed to her reward in the Year of Grace 1831. My father and two older brothers remain, tho I have not shared their company in three years' time. Sisters I have none. I am an apprentice stonecutter. My master is Mr. Charles Bonness.

No, that will not do either. These words are true enough, but as the Reverend Yates has said, the truth and the facts are not always the same. If this journal is to contain an accurate story of my life, then I will strive for the truth and not merely the facts.

September 5

A remarkable day! Today I was allowed, at last, to cut a stone with no assistance or superintendence by Mr. Bonness. This is indeed a day of note, when my work here begins a new season. Tho I am still an apprentice, Mr. Bonness has placed trust in me that I hope I shall not disappoint.

Three years now I have been sharpening stone-saws, scoring and flaking the broad blocks of marble, grinding chisel points. Three years now I've hauled water and mucked the out-barn where Nessie and Chloe are kept. Three years I've taken instruction at the knee of Mr. Bonness. But today I am less a boy and more a man.

I have labored on a good six dozen gravemarkers since Mr. Bonness taught me to hold the chisel thus and strike in the tap-tap-tap three-stroke pattern with my hammer. But always this work was under his eye and direction.

However, today he said to me, "Albion, we have much work. The misfortune of others is a fortune for us." And he gave me leave to select a block and set to cutting.

It is a small stone. But no death is small for those left behind. The father of the babe has requested we make an angel on the front side. For this I am glad. I much enjoy the fine feathery work of the wings. We were also given this word to inscribe:

Lo death steps in.
The solemn stroke is given.
She sighs. She falls asleep.
She mounts to heaven.

This is a fine sentiment, but for a babe not yet one year of age still a hard and mournful saying. Tho my labors keep me ever in the company of bereft parents, widows, and widowers, I think it not always so gloomful a profession to follow. For we make things of beauty. Angels, lambs, doves, upward-pointing fingers, willows. Even some of the death's heads that Mr. Bonness has carved have a certain dread wonder. My Heavenly Maker has smiled on me, to give such a profession when other boys my age are haying or plowing or cutting endless ricks of firewood.

My work is most pleasurable. I do love the clink of the hammer on the chisel-head like a steady drumbeat. I love the cloud of rock dust that hangs in the air after a long day's work. And when the sun slants through the dust like a smoky beam from heaven it gives me such happiness. The brilliant sparks that fly from the flinty slabs, too, are a joy. Most of all, I love to see the forms arising from the rough stone blocks like a face coming forth from a stewy fog. Our tools are cold and hard but they can make a softness, if our skills prevail, out of sandstone and marble and slate. The angel faces, these I carve with great happiness. How many yet have I helped to fashion? And how many more will I create before I am called from this world?

September 7

I slept poorly last night, Little Watty making all types of noises in his slumber. He talks from dreams, making nonsense, even singing a little in his sleep.

I should never complain. How many other apprentice boys sleep in the home of the master? I could well have expected Mr. Bonness to fit me up a garret over the stone shop. But from the day I began with him, he has treated me with great kindness. I've eaten at the table with the family, and Mrs. Bonness has even at times sewn a new shirt for me or baked me a sweetmeat as tho I were her natural son. While it's Watty who bears the Bonness name and not I, there are times when it seems Mr. Bonness has greater affection for me. It's not that Watty is less loved, but that his peculiarity doesn't allow his parents to draw near. And he shows no talent for stonecutting. This, I'm sure, is a burden for my master. To have a son follow in his footsteps is certainly what every artisan hopes for.

Watty made baleful noises last night in his dreams. At last I could bear the sound no longer and shook him awake. He gasped and clung to me in bed, then, seeing it was I, grew calmer.

"I heard the trumpet calling," he said. When I asked what trumpet, he shook and even wept a bit. "The trumpet. I hear it most nights now. The trumpet call long as the river. Sad and lonely, like a girl's wailing. But deeper." He went on in this vein, hardly making sense. "A bull might moan this way, trapped down in the swampy flats. But it was no beast I heard."

I pulled back the window curtain and we sat on the bed together, looking out at the moonlit sky. An oak leaned her branches against the side of the house, but that night there was no wind and no scraping sound. I heard nothing. But Watty sat, still listening.

Usually he is glib and merry about the sounds he hears. This night, however, there was fear in him. "Why am I the only one who hears it?" he whispered. "If it were the Trump of Doom, then it would blast only once." I'd heard tell of the certain religionists, followers of Father Miller to the east of us, who claim that the end of this world is nigh, that they have predicted the date with precision.

"It's like a moan, Albion, a hurt and lonely moan. Seven nights now I've heard it. Once just as we got into bed. Once at dawn. Once at midnight. The peepers saw away like fiddlers in the dark. A quiet sound. It makes me sleep. But then the trumpet blast comes."

A summons, I knew some would say. A call. But who was calling Watty?

Perhaps it's merely the power of mental fancy. Watty was much taken with the stone his father has been working on of late: a large marker with the angel Gabriel blowing his trumpet, calling the dead to rise up from the ground.

"If I could carve like you, Albion, I would make that trumpet. I would fashion it in hard stone and then it would no longer plague me in my sleep."

September 7 (later)

Three outlandish men have come into town and are staying next door at Mr. Miles's Inn. I worked until sunset last night on a door sill and heard all manner of noisy song and speechifying. Mr. Miles often keeps disorderly guests, but it seems that these three men have the stormiest tongues I'd ever heard. I'd have guessed them drunk on Mr. Miles's whiskey but for a smatter of the words I caught.

I saw them at the dinner hour burst out from the tavern. One wears a long beard and such a fearsome look on his face. His voice booms like a cannon and his two followers — indeed such they seemed by their fawning and lesser manner — echo back his words.

I'd been hooking the block and tackle to Nessie, to hoist the sill stone onto our wagon, and struggling too, for Watty was nowhere to be seen, when the three men made their presence known. From their odd accents and garb I guessed them to be canalmen, for I'd heard that some of those had come from hundreds of miles hence and were known for their heathenish ways.

Their leader caught sight of me as I yanked the hoist chains, and he shouted for me to lay it by. I kept at my work, harder now with Nessie uneasy from the loud and harsh parlaying so near. The men marched toward me and their leader told me to cease from my labors.

I tried to keep the hoist chains out of his grasp, but he was joined by his men and they set the stone to swinging back and forth like a pendulum on a clock. "Such is the soul," the bearded one shouted. "Now this way and now that, swinging wild from east to west." Nessie was frantic, jerking the wagon forward and back, and making a loud protest.

Then, all of a sudden, the man with the beard saw inside our workshop and let go of the chain. The stone dropped to the earth like God's plummet, but thankfully did not crack or chip. The man pushed by me and saw the half-completed gravemarker that I had begun just a few days before.

His cohorts joined him inside our shop. All their loudness and hilarity was gone now.

For a reason I don't understand, I didn't want the men to see the angel I'd been working on, as tho their eyes would somehow defile her. I didn't want their loud voices reading the words of the inscription.

I moved to one side, between the lantern's light and the angel stone, protecting her.

"You made this, boy?"

I nodded, and the man fixed me with his milky blue eyes. He came closer to the stone, and a measure of his hardness seemed to melt. He reached out to touch the angel's face, and I slapped his hand away. He snarled, low and long, as if a hungry beast who'd been denied his meat. The other men came quickly to his aid, pulling me away from him.

"Never, never touch him," one of the men hissed, like a king's lackey shooing off a pesky peasant. Indeed, I hoped never to see him, let alone come close enough to feel again his cool snaky skin.

"This is good, boy. You are skilled with the chisel and hammer," the bearded one said. "You have been given a great gift." He stroked two fingers over the angel's forehead, nodding and murmuring what sounded like a prayer. Then he turned abruptly and stalked off with his men.

I stood a long time in the shop, close by the angel, looking at her face. In the light from the lantern, it seemed that the marble was marred and stained by the man's touch.

September 8

I asked Mr. Bonness what he knew of the three strange men. Other than old Edward Blackpool, who had marched as far as Philadelphia and Baltimore during our War of Independence, Mr. Bonness knows more of the wide world than anyone here in Little Sion. He was born in Connecticut, like many folks here around, but had followed the sea for years, then located and learned the trade of stonecutting. If anyone knew what to make of the strangers, I'd wager it would be him.

"They are traveling through," he said, while we wrestled a block of marble into the cutting cradle. "Wayfarers."

But what kind of men are they? I thought I'd heard someone in town, mayhaps Sarah Williams's mother, use the word "Prophet." Were they men of God? How could they be, with such fiery tongues and disorderly manner?

"There," Mr. Bonness said, rocking the block into place. "There. We'll need to make short work of this. There are more jobs waiting."

I didn't want to shirk from my labor, but I felt that if I didn't understand what kind of men the three strangers were, I couldn't keep my mind on my work. I asked again.

"Albion, your curiosity has more than once taken you where you didn't want to be. It's a good property of mind, to yearn for understanding. But these men are best forgotten. I want you to promise me you won't go around them, asking and prying after their business."

I told Mr. Bonness that last night I had fairly hidden from the men, but they would not let me be. "Were they drunken?" I asked.

"Not on whiskey or strong cider."

This answer, of course, made me want to know more. What else, besides spirituous liquors, could make a man drunk?

Sighing, Mr. Bonness sat down on a heap of unfinished door sills. "Albion, this is a season of strange happenings. And York State seems to have more than its fair share. You know about the revivals led by Charles Finney, how the folks fall moaning and crying to the floor. Even here in Little Sion news of that kind reaches us. But there are other currents running in the stream. You've heard of Joseph Smith, up at Palmyra, how he discovered a Golden Bible and gathered believers before he set off to the west. And over toward Cayuga, a good thirty miles, there was the lady-prophet who called herself the 'Publick and Universal Friend.' This part of the world is full of those yearning folks. We live in hard times, and people want something to make their travail a little easier."

So then the three men were indeed prophets?

"I don't know for certain, Albion. I have no truck with such things. But I am sure that these men are filled with a strange spirit. It is not for us to decide whether it is of God or His enemy. I want you to steer a clear course around them, however long they tarry here. With a fair share of luck, they'll be gone this morrow and we can get back to our work with no more distraction." He stood and handed me a sheaf of chisels. "These all need to be ground. And then hie yourself down to Bill Cotton and bring me back the chain he's promised me a week now."

I did as I was told. I knew we had no time for jawing. Even if we worked without ceasing a week straight, we couldn't have gotten all our promised jobs done. I want Mr. Bonness to trust me. I want him to know I'm a good worker and true.

September 8 (continued)

I swung the hammer until my arms ached and my ears rang. I cut and I cut, and by eventide there was a heap of fine rubble and three goodly mantelpieces. And then I got to work again on my angel face.

But I suppose that was not the right course of action, for no sooner had I chipped a half dozen times than the bearded man appeared in the shop. I had three lanterns burning, hanging from the ceiling beams. They were good tin lanterns with fat tallow candles inside. But the man appeared in the light like a ghost, there and not there. He stared at me, as if to beckon.

"Mr. Bonness is not here," I told him. But I knew he had not come to see my master.

He approached my gravestone angel quietly. Alone, all of his disorderly ways seemed to have fled. He was somber, the way a mother or father is somber when they see their child lowered into the ground.

"I had an angel," he said at last. "But she's gone." He touched the face again, gently. "You must have seen her, too, for you've caught her face exactly."

I tried to speak, but his presence seemed to draw the air out of the shop. His eyes turned toward me, and I knew what a block of stone must feel when two powerful chisels are aimed at its heart. "What is your name, boy?"

My silence seemed to kindle his anger. "I am not one to trifle with, boy." One hand clenched the other, squeezing all the color away.

I did not want him to know my name, as if telling would give him some power over me.

By the fierce look he gave me, it was clear he was not accustomed to men — let alone boys — denying his commands. He did not threaten me harm, not with his words. He did not say what punishments he was wont to use, but I could well imagine his hand on the drover's whip.

"Tell me your name."

"Albion Straight," I whispered.

His wrath ebbed away.

"Your work is good. Your work is true." Then he reached and touched me on the forehead, two fingers pressing. I listed to one side, grasping at the wall to keep myself from swooning away. The air, of a sudden, tasted bright and sweet, as when the peppermint harvest comes in and the whole town of Little Sion is perfumed.

But was this a sign of blessing he made on my forehead, or was he marking me as a sheep is marked by the fiery brand?

Then he was gone, and I righted myself. But I could barely lift the hammer. And now, as I write these words, the goose quill itself feels like a bar of iron, and the knife I use to keep it trim is like a mighty sword.

The three men are gone and Little Sion is back to its usual ways. Bill Cotton labors at his forge, with his boy

Jimmy working the bellows steady as clockwork. The Reverend Mr. Yates is about, today visiting Mrs. Tweed, whose girl Samantha is gravely ill. The young scholars straggle to school, chattering and wild as monkeys.

But Mr. Miles's tavern is far quieter now. Not just because the three travelers are no longer there making a ruckus, but because the place feels their absence. Something has happened here in Little Sion, tho I'm sure no one here could say exactly what it was.

September 10

Little Watty disappeared today and has left Mrs. Bonness in a perfect state of distraction. It's of no note when a boy of eleven years goes off by himself to the woods. However, Watty was dire sick last night, fevering and sweaty as a washrag. He said the most outlandish things in his delirium. The comet has disordered his mind, I fear.

Mrs. Bonness had him down in the main room most of the night with compresses on his head. Near dawn, so she told me, the fever seemed to break. She let him sleep in the trundle bed in her room. The work of the house got on: my master and I down to the shop and his wife at the loom she keeps in the back room. It makes a great noise, whooshing and clacking, steady, as they say the ocean waves are steady.

When she went to bring Watty some milkbread for his breakfast, she found the bed empty.

Tho the demand for our work has increased twofold in the last few months, still Mr. Bonness and I were sent a-hunting for Watty. I knew most of his haunts and went first to those places.

The old shanty up above Green Lick is mostly fallen in by now, log walls and rough-hewn slabs for a roof. The one little window, however, Watty used to much enjoy looking through. It was made of bottles laid on end and cemented around with moss and clay. When the sun hangs at the right angle, Watty said, the light shines through like a dozen strands of fire. I poked about in the hut, but saw no sign of him and didn't tarry long.

Next I hied myself down to Chambers Creek. I didn't cry out his name, for he had better ears than anyone I'd ever known and creeping up on him unawares was impossible. I sat only a moment on a broad flat rock of granite. The sun burnt unusual warm for an autumn day. Dragonflies buzzed in the hot air, almost as loud as the burble of the creek.

Then I went on to the hollow where Billy Drummond claimed to have seen a panther, then to the crest of Ackland's Hill, whence you can look a few miles to the west and see the Genesee winding through the broad-shouldered valley.

At last I made my way to the cleared-out place on the backside of Sam Carol's farm, where last year there'd been a mighty time of revival. I went out to the camp meeting only once. It was at night time, and the clearing was ringed with torches all around. Some boys perched up in the oaks with their brands burning, and the light quaked and throbbed a terrible red. The people were in full cry when I came there, singing a sacred song about the last trumpet blow. They were so loud, so raucous, that I thought the noise itself might call the dead up from their beds of clay. And then the preacher, with a voice as strong as a hickory whip, thrashed the crowd. They were much taken by his words, some falling onto the ground, some overcome with the jerks. It was a powerful time, and many a sinner was brought under God's mercy that night.

But today the cleared place is empty. The weeds are grown up some, tho I could see the spots where the wagons had rutted the damp ground. In the fire pits ringing the clearing there were a few bits of trash. I found a nail and a spoon and broken saucer. The preacher's platform was still there, and mostly in good order. It stood a man's height off the ground and was covered on top with a rough-shingled roof. Now empty, in the broad afternoon daylight, it seemed another place entirely from the revival ground of last year. With no one watching me, I thought to climb up the little ladder and survey the ground from the vantage point of the preacher.

I stood in the campground pulpit, feeling a little of the power which had run through the preacher that night. Where the weeds now blew, a hundred believers had rocked and moaned and sang. Out on the edges of the circle had been a score of wagons, some folks traveling here from as far as fifty miles hence.

"Amen, brother!" A voice came from far off, as if echoing from last year. Again I heard it: "Amen."

I wanted to hide, but there on the platform it felt the whole world could see me. A small voice, a boy's voice.

A third time: "Amen," and then Watty came out of his hiding place in a stand of scrubby pines.

"Your mother is half crazy sick with worry!" I shouted down at him, as if I were the preacher and I was telling a sinner to repent.

He clapped his hands, delighted, I suppose, to see me made such a monkey. He walked toward the preaching stand slow and steady, keeping me fixed with his eyes.

"Walter Bonness, your mother is bereft with worry. We need to go back right now," I shouted down at him. Then, feeling foolish there in the preacher's stand, I clambered down and took Watty by the arm.

As I marched him back to town, Watty told me what he'd done and where he'd been that day. His face was still flushed and his eyes shiny bright. I think the fever was still in him, and this was making him so full of talk.

Much of it was a pranking boy's prattle. I didn't pay it much mind. But as we passed Youngmans' farm, the last one before town, Watty began talking about the three wayfarers.

"Simeon Coombs told me they were canalers. But

that's not true. And I heard two girls whispering that the men were prophets like Father Miller or Joe Smith or Mathias. But that's a lie, too. I was Listening Hard two nights ago when Papa told you to stay a fair good distance away from the men."

When Watty hears what no one else can he calls it Listening Hard. Some folks in town say its trickery, but I know better. He might have been in the house or well down to the Proctors' field and still heard Mr. Bonness's warning.

"So then who do you say they are?" I asked.

Watty went off rattling about other topics, just to spite my interest.

"Tell me, Watty, who are they?" We stopped at the old dry well. Much farther and everyone in the village would see that Watty was back. And he'd be swarmed over, and I wouldn't get another word out of him for days.

"You were Listening Hard, weren't you Watty? You were hiding in the dark by the tavern and you were listening to what the men said when they were all by themselves. And you know all about them." That wasn't a question. And Watty didn't bother to say yes to it.

"There are two who follow and one who leads."

That was clear to anyone who saw them. But Watty knew more.

"The stoop-shouldered one is called Walter, like me. The other follower is named Boot. But they're not important really. It's the one with the beard who you need to mind, Albion."

Just then Samantha Jones spotted us and let out a whoop, and in an eyeblink the whole town was on us shouting and asking a hundred questions.

Watty paid a price for the trick he played on his mother. But not so severe a price. Mrs. Bonness says "spare the rod and spoil the child," but she could never switch her boy. She has a big bundle of birch gads that she threatens to lick him with, but Watty is too precious to punish much. It was just before I came to be apprenticed that Watty's twin sisters both died of the scarlet fever. I never heard either Mr. or Mrs. Bonness talk about the little girls, but I have seen the beautiful gravestone he carved for them and asked around town and that's how I know.

It's well past late and my candle is guttering out. No more writing tonight.

September 12

No entry yesterday. We worked from sunup to almost midnight, and my arms ached so I could barely hold the knife to trim my quill.

Mr. Bonness considers taking on another apprentice. He said it won't be long 'til I'm a journeyman, I've learned so much already. It gave me a pause, and I might say hurt a little mite to think of another boy taking my place here in the stoneyard. I don't want to leave, even if I do learn all Mr. Bonness has to teach me.

He's said that business will just get better. We can float our work north on arks, and at Rochester it can be bought by agents and sent either west or east on the Erie. Another boy would be useful with all the new houses and commercial buildings going up in the cities along the canal. There's a goodly market for sills and mantelpieces and the like.

Mr. Bonness has said that it's a shame to keep me on the cruder hewing work when I could be doing carvings on gravestones and perhaps someday a memorial to a hero of the republic. I've heard that there's a full-sized carving of General Washington in Albany. How I'd love to see that! Mr. Bonness has even seen the great monument to our first president in the nation's capital. It shows him seated with one arm upraised, dressed in the garb of a Roman senator. My good master told me the statue is two or three times life-size, carved from excellent marble, and gives anyone who sees it a shiver of pride. I doubt the man who carved that started out in a place like Little Sion, however. Mr. Bonness said it was carved by an American, but the man must have studied in Italy where all the great stonecutters are found.

September 13

Mr. Bonness gave me leave to work today on the angel. She's almost done now, an airy little being. Tho there's still much to learn, I think that this is good work. Mr. Bonness has been watching my progress and tho he never smiles, I can tell that he approves. Work that is shoddy or merely good enough he pays little mind to. But I can see him now and again looking over at me as I work, and once I saw him staring at the angel's face when he thought he was alone.

She hovers over the ground, light as a moonbeam. It gives me great joy to take such a heavy material as marble and transform it into an image that floats. And it pleases Mr. Bonness that the stone will be planted somewhere near enough that we can see it now and again. "Your first fine work," he said. "You'll want to go back in your latter life and examine it. I'll wager that some day you'll be a great stonecutter, and people will know your name well beyond Little Sion and even York State. Mayhaps folks will come and see this stone and say 'This is where Albion Straight had his beginning.' "

With this kind of praise it is difficult to keep working. One sloppy hammer stroke, one lazy placement of the chisel, and my angel becomes nothing. Worse tho is the thought that I might disappoint Mr. Bonness. Seeing disapproval on his face hurts me more than anything.

September 14

Another wayfarer has come to town, tho not as strange as the three men last week. He is dressed more respectable, and I hear none of the sounds of drunken dramming from the tavern. He has a faraway look about him, like a man who can see a glimpse of heaven.

He's round about the middle, and he plasters his hair flat down on his head. I imagine he doesn't work in the field. Perhaps he is a lawyer or a doctor. But his boots are well worn, like those of a man who's come a very long way in his travels. His name is William Williams.

September 15

A very remarkable day! I've found out who Mr. Williams is and why he's come to Little Sion.

He spent much of the afternoon in conference with my master. I was sent a good ten miles to take delivery on a load of Vermont marble shipped across the Erie and then carted down from Rochester. But we could have gone for the stone any day. Watty and I were sent away, I suppose, so that Mr. Bonness could speak freely with his guest.

When I arrived back in the village, Mr. Williams was still at the house. Mr. Bonness came out and told me leave the stone in the wagon for later. "We have news for you, Albion. A proposition." He shook my hand, which he never did, as tho I were a man now and not just a boy apprentice.

We came into the sitting room and Mr. Williams rose. I was covered with dust and clay, and my left hand was bloody and bandaged with rags, for I'd slipped earlier and smashed my thumb.

But before I could go to the pump to clean myself off, I was ushered into the sitting room.

"Albion, Mr. Williams has need of a stonecutter. He's come here to Little Sion to inquire about hiring me out. I told him that was impossible. I can't give up a month here. But when I showed him your work in the shop, he was delighted and inquired if your services were for hire. I told him they were, but that you'd have to agree."

I asked what he wanted from me.

Mr. Williams spoke in a thin quavering voice, as tho he were sick with fever. This was odd from such a robust and round man. But his words were not unkind.

"You are skilled well beyond your years, Albion. I came to Little Sion because I knew the reputation of your master. But I think you are the man to do the work I need."

He pointed to a sheaf of papers on the table. "This chart shows the lands of Mr. John Augustus Good. I have the happy fortune to be his personal agent in matters of finance. He has established his estate here." Mr. Williams pointed to a spot of white on the map. His pudgy finger pointed, but I understood nothing. The places of York State where I'd never been were all a mystery to me. Rochester might have been as far off as London. And the great city of Manhattan could have been situated in China. I was born only fifteen miles from Little Sion and had traveled no more than that distance in all my life.

"This is the Genesee River," Mr. Williams said, tracing his finger on a wiggling line. "And this is Mr. Good's domain."

I told him I didn't understand.

"Albion, Mr. Good is building his estate on these

lands. Perhaps not as great as the manors of the Livingstons and Rensalears along the Hudson River, but for this area, it will be a marvel. And he desires that certain stonework be fashioned for his house and adjoining properties. To entice a stonecutter from New York City is impossible. And your master has said he can't leave his home for such an extended period of time. But he suggested that perhaps you might consent."

Consent! He was asking a boy if he'd consent to work for such a great man. Of course I looked to Mr. Bonness for his word. He nodded and smiled. "It is your choice, Albion. You can stay here if you'd like. Or you can go with Mr. Williams and do the work he has for you."

I asked how long I'd be away.

"That depends on a number of factors. Mr. Good's needs have not been established in their particulars. But I'd say three months away. Perhaps four or five. Then you could return here and take up your work again. Of course your payment would depend on the length of time you served."

Payment! I'd never earned a penny for my work. My bed and board and training in the stonecutter's craft were all I earned. And this was more than I deserved. But to be paid in real money for my work was a thing hard to consider.

"He's offering a hundred dollars, Albion. A hundred dollars for three months' work. And another twenty-five for every month you work beyond that."

I was shocked by such an offer, of course. Boys who work out on a farm for three years are given the sum of one hundred dollars on their twenty-first birthday when their contract ends. Three years or three months for the same amount of money. I knew not how to respond, the news was so astonishing.

"I'm sure you'll need some time to consider it, Albion," Mr. Williams said. "Do you think that you can give me an answer tomorrow?"

I looked to Mr. Bonness. My time with him had been the happiest of my life, without doubt. The prospect of giving up his company grieved me. But a hundred dollars was a strong temptation, as was the chance to do work for such a man as Mr. Good.

"Will you have an answer for me on the morrow?"

"No," I said.

Frowns and dark looks all around.

"No," I said again. "I can give you an answer tonight."

I went to Mr. Bonness and took his hand. "Is this a task that you wish me to undertake?"

He nodded.

"Then I will do it."

I write these words now with the candle flickering low and Watty talking in his sleep beside me. Three months, perhaps more, I'll be gone. This gives me deep uneasiness. But Mr. Bonness has said he wishes it, and I will trust that he knows best for me.

September 18

So much has happened in the last three days. I've had no time for my journal.

First, Mr. Bonness said he wanted me to sleep on my decision. I agreed but knew that there'd be no change. If he thought it best for me, then I would do it. That night, after Mr. Williams returned to the inn, I wrote the last entry. But after midnight some time Watty jerked upright from the trundle bed and called to me in the dark.

"Albion, Albion! Do you hear it?"

I was hardly awake, still tangled up in the night's dreams. "Hear what?"

"That cry. Like a girl but no girl. There! It comes again."

I listened hard and long, but heard nothing beside the sighing of the wind.

"You've been dreaming again."

We stayed up for a while, talking about Mr. Williams and his proposal. Watty said he was afraid for me, but I took that as a childish way of telling me how much he'd miss me. I hated to leave Little Sion, and the kindness of the Bonness household, but such an opportunity, my master told me, would likely never come again. Certainly not for such a young man. I had always trusted Mr. Bonness's judgment, and I would continue.

"Things are not what they appear to be," Watty whispered.

I asked what he meant, and he said he didn't know. "But I'm afraid, Albion."

The next day Mr. Bonness and I went to the inn to give Mr. Williams my formal acceptance. He'd already drawn up the contract, and after my master had read the terms and deemed them acceptable, I signed. Then came packing and preparations. Tools, food, clothing, another book for me to keep my journal in. "You'll want to put your thoughts down, Albion. And perhaps others will want to read them some day."

Mrs. Bonness said I couldn't bid her goodbye until she'd finished a new shirt, and so she sewed all the day. Watty buzzed around like an inquisitive fly, asking a hundred questions, none of which I could answer: How long would it take to reach the Good estate? How many others were already living there? Where had Mr. Good made his fortune? Were there other artisans already there working?

"You had better take Nessie," Mr. Bonness said. "To carry your tools and bags. And she knows you and won't balk at the hoist lines. I'm sure Mr. Good has other draft beasts, but Nessie knows you and has grown used to the work."

I tried to persuade Mr. Bonness that this was out of the question. How could he continue his work with only Chloe? But he said he could use others' horses in share. "Old man Branetree has said he'd loan me his team if I needed one. It's fine, Albion. You take Nessie, and you bring her back in three months."

So it was on the eighteenth day of September 1835 that I, Albion Straight, set off on my journey southward, in the company of Mr. William Williams. Most of the town came out to give me the parting hand. Such tears from Mrs. Bonness, as tho I were her only son and she were losing him forever. Watty trotted along beside us, saying farewell again and again. The crowd thinned, and Mr. and Mrs. Bonness disappeared, and soon only Watty was left. Then he, too, gave a final goodbye.

We traveled long that day, the road soon withering to a trail. We kept near the river when we could, with the sun on our right shoulder. We made camp near to dusk, and I write these words now by the light of a fire.

September 19

The wilderness deepens. We've seen no man nor woman all day. I'm not afraid, but a certain uneasiness does trouble my heart. We are now well beyond the farthest point south I've ever gone. We've seen the smoke from two chimneys, and once I believe I heard a boy's voice. But we are very much alone in this place.

Mr. Williams is a strange man. At times he is as quiet and unyielding as a limestone block. I ask him questions about Mr. John Good. I ask about the estate he's building. I ask about its location and whether I might get any kind of communication back to Little Sion while I'm there. And his answer is no answer. He rides along as blank faced as a dead man.

But then something will seem to prick him, and he fills the forest with his quaking voice, which sounds to me like a fiddle played by a palsied old man. "There are very important tasks to be accomplished, Mr. Straight." He never calls me by my first name. It is strange to my ear to be addressed so. "Your efforts will not be just of a decorative nature but will contribute to an endeavor of most passing greatness. You should understand yourself a most fortunate young man, to be chosen by Mr. Good for this work." I didn't think I'd been chosen by Mr. Good, but perhaps as his agent, Mr. Williams considers himself as eyes and ears and hands of the great man.

I asked then, again, how long it would take us to reach Mr. Good's lands.

The answer was a barking kind of cough, sharp and hard. He looked over and fixed me with a rheumy-eyed stare. "Soon enough we'll be there," he said and would say no more.

We are sitting now at our fire, and the darkness looms around as baleful as the walls of a cave. We hear the night beasts moving, crying at times, and a certain wild shrill note comes at what seems a regular interval, like the workings of a clock which tells out the time. We've boiled our little portion of bacon, eaten our goodnight bread, and now wait for sleep. Having never traveled far, I'm unable to judge the distance we've gone. Since the sun was at noon, we saw not a single cabin or shanty. The fire is guttering out and it becomes more difficult to write.

September 20

Another long day of travel, but today Mr. Williams spoke more and this lifted the forest gloom a bit.

At times his talk was as strange and disordered as

Little Watty's midnight rambling. I recognized in his discourse the name Swedenborg, who I believe is a renowned philosopher. He made references to spirits, but whether he meant liquors or angels I couldn't determine. And what he says about Mr. John Augustus Good does not put my heart at ease.

"He is a great man, but not as others are great. Wealth does not guarantee greatness. Nor does walking in the halls of power like a judge or senator. Having a thousand followers means nothing if the words you lead them with are mere beautiful puffs of air." He slapped his horse, not to goad her on, but to capture my attention completely. "Mr. Straight, it is of utmost importance that you understand the gravity of our mission. You have contracted a three-month period of service to Mr. Good, but you may find that it will last a lifetime."

I asked what he meant, and he repeated himself. When I asked for an explanation, he was mum. We rode a few miles in silence. The trail here has shrunk to almost nothing. We go slower now, having to find ways around too-deep streams and too-steep hillsides. Nessie is unused to this kind of travel, and I must confess that I am not either.

For a man attired as he is in frock coat and city-bought breeches, for a round-bellied and weakly-voiced person, Mr. Williams is surprisingly skillful at wilderness travel.

We skirted a wide bog this afternoon. The mosquitoes tormented us, and the stink from the dead water was awful, odious as a drunkard's belch. But we put that foul place behind us, and, cresting a hill, got a view down to the river.

"Do you know why they call this the Genesee?" Mr. Williams asked.

Getting my negative reply, he explained that in the tongue of the Iroquois the word *Genesee* means "beautiful valley." Certainly here that is true. The sun was coming down in a welter of red and orange and yellow. Great whorls and masses of crimson-painted clouds hung over the western ridge. I wondered if I would ever have the skill to capture such a scene in carved stone. We have no color to work with, just shape and size and what Mr. Bonness calls "texture." We can make the stone smooth as a looking glass, or rippled as a creek in a windstorm. We can make it pebbly or streaky or knobby. Perhaps someday, I thought, looking at the beautiful red-shot sky, I could give that impression in cold stone.

September 21

We saw other persons today, and as the rain came down heavy, we inquired if we might tarry with them for the night.

The shanty was barely the size of the sitting room in the Bonness home. And the family inhabiting it were six strong. A man, rather grim and haggard, his wife who worked almost constantly at her little loom, and four girls lived there. Still they agreed to put us up and give us a jot of food.

It was a dismal little place, and it grieved me to see the lives these four girls were to endure. There would be no apprenticeship for any of them, no escape to happier endeavors. They will live in the shanty until they find husbands and then toil as their mother does at the smoking fireplace and the spinning wheel.

The youngest now totters around on the dirt floor of the shanty, happily prattling to herself. She seems to find joy in our company. And tho Mr. Williams has said not three words to the girl, she gives him her smile and her sweet childish talk.

"I Lila, I Lila," she says again and again, hoping for a smile or acknowledging nod.

"I am Albion," I say, and she comes to cling at my knee while I write. The other girls all have handwork, and they sit huddled on a log bench before the spluttering firelight.

Mr. Crane — for this is the family name — has not asked why we've traveled so distant from the main routes. They go at fortnightly stretches without seeing anyone on the trail, but Mr. Crane keeps a solemn silence.

We ate venison this night, and a little corn cake, and a few handfuls of dried strawberries. Lila whined and begged, but her father would give her nothing but the back of his hand. We were to pay for our bed and board that night, and it pleased me to sneak a berry to the little girl while her father was poking angrily at the coals of the fire.

The Autumnal Equinox

Strange, very strange, tidings. We are no longer alone on our journey.

After we left the Crane homestead and had wended a few miles along a meandering track, we heard a call from afar. Much to my amaze, Mr. Williams rooted in his sidepack and pulled forth a small tin dinner horn. He gave three short blasts, and the alarm was answered by three longer hoots.

I asked what this meant, but he kept his silence, fixing his eyes on the forest shadow.

Soon we forded a bright chattering stream, and, as we clambered our horses up the rocky bank, we heard the three noises again, much closer.

Mr. Williams played out loud again on his tin horn.

I was sore afraid now, admitting what I'd not allowed myself yet to think: that Mr. Williams had lured me away from Little Sion and meant some grave harm. I pulled Nessie around to head back along the track to the Cranes' farmhold. They were not welcoming nor happy folk, but surely they'd give me sanctuary.

"No," Mr. Williams said at last. "Don't go. They are here."

He pointed and there in the trail were three figures.

Now my fear turned to most passing astonishment. For there, only a few rods down the trail, were the three wayfarers who'd tarried in Little Sion. The Bearded One held up his hand in a sign of greeting. The others, too, saluted us. Mr. Williams dismounted of a sudden and told me to do the same. I hesitated, thinking I might spur Nessie and outrun this strange gathering of men.

"No," he said, "Stay. Get down off her. You can't greet your new master mounted. It isn't fitting."

Mr. Williams grabbed Nessie's bridle rope and again told me to dismount. I might still have bolted, but my gaze went to the Bearded One, who was now approaching. His great watery blue eyes met mine, and I felt his power. I did as I was told. The others came behind as retainers follow a nobleman. Mr. Williams bowed a greeting.

He took my hand and then the hand of the Bearded One. "Albion Straight, this is your new master, Mr. John Augustus Good."

"The stonecutter, the one who can make angels out

of cold marble," the Bearded One said. "You've heard the summons and obeyed. It is good, as I am Good." He took my hand in both of his, and squeezed, not as men greet each other but as a lord claiming his new vassal.

He is a powerful man, tho older than Mr. Bonness. His beard is gray and white, like iron and ice. Still, there is a heat about him, as tho a furnace were burning in his heart.

I asked why they had brought me thither.

"As you were told: I have need of your services," John Good said. "I came to Little Sion because I'd heard your master's work praised. I examined certain of his gravecarvings, at Temple Hill in Chenusio, at the church yards in Groveland and Sonyea. I came to engage his services. But upon seeing your work, I knew at once you were the one I sought."

"We need to go back," I said. "I must return to Little Sion and discuss this with my master."

"That is not possible now." He still held my hand, and I knew what a slave must feel with the iron shackles weighing him down. "You will accompany me to Goodspell — that is the name I have established for my new home. You will fulfill your contract, working the three months at my behest. Only then will you be free to return."

One of his followers had taken hold of Nessie. The other had moved around to block the trail back. John Good squeezed my hand again, hard enough to hurt. But even when he let go, I was still a prisoner.

We rode on, heading south, for another few hours. We made camp beside a waterfall, which prattles now like a little child. I was afraid for the men to see my journal, afraid they might take it away. But I asked leave to write in it, and John Good seemed pleased.

"A young man of letters! This is excellent. Other than my secretary, Williams, none of the other folk you'll meet at Goodspell can write more than their own name. By all means, by all means, put down your thoughts." Then he shouted for Boot, one of his followers, to build up the fire so I would see better.

September 23

In the night I thought I heard a panther crying. It was a baleful, terrible sound. And it made me think of Watty, all alone now, listening at the window. We kept the fire burning all night, to ward off the beasts.

We rose and set off with the dawn. Our travel is mostly silent. No one speaks unless his master speaks first.

It seemed that we must have crossed the Pennsylvania line by now. But when I asked, John Good said no. "Our progress is slower here than before. The trail to Goodspell winds around like a knotted rope."

I certainly am lost. The forest is thick here. No farms do we see. Only an occasional shanty built into the side of a hill. But not once today, another person nor a plume of smoke from the chimney.

I've never in my life been this alone. Even before I came under Mr. Bonness's rule, I had some companionship. My father was often gone and my brothers with him, stripping bark to sell to the tannery at Nunda, or cutting shingles at the Black Creek camp. After my mother's death the house was a dreary place, and I think my father wished to stay away. Still, I lived then with kin, even if they were hard and silent men.

Now, I travel with strangers, unsure even where I am. I have a trade to follow and an employer who requires my services. But I am alone as I have never been alone before.

Some say the panther cries at night to find his mate. Others have told me he cries to warn off his enemies. But I think I understand better. Listening to his far-off wail last night I knew why he cried. He is alone, and his dreadful solitude grieves his heart.

September 24

We've reached our destination at last. I had pictured a beautiful house and gardens. I had expected broad fields of hay and corn and barns overflowing. I saw the Wadsworth's estate once, with the pastures dotted by huge ancient oaks.

Goodspell is none of these. There is shelter, and it will be good to sleep tonight under a roof. But this is a strange and confusing place. At first all that I saw were shanties and log huts, a pen for sheep and a ramshackly hay barn. But as we passed through this place I saw farther down the muddy track the half-finished mansion house. Huge beams jutted this way and that like the bones of a dead giant. Piles of stone and lumber were heaped around the house. Closer, I heard the rumble of a mill. There is a creek here, which supplies power for the cutting of timbers. A wagon rattled by, and the driver tipped his hat to John Good, as a countryman would show respect for the squire.

He is not just landlord here. That is most clear. The way others bow and lower their eyes, speak with a groveling tone, tells me much about John Good. He has might, beyond that which wealth or book-learning or bodily strength gives a man.

We stopped in front of the mansion house, and he pointed proudly. "When it is completed, Goodspell will be the largest building in the county. Bigger than any church, bigger than the courthouse. But there's still much work to be done."

I asked where I would be employed.

"We'll need sills and mantelpieces, door thresholds and chimneys. But you can oversee my boys in that regard. I have hopes you'll have them trained up in that simple labor within a week."

"Then I can go home?" A pang of joy pierced me like an arrow of delight.

He smiled broadly, not with happiness but a kind of

cruel mirth. "Of course not. I didn't bring you here for such simple work. There are far more important labors that await you." He took my hands and inspected them as I would inspect a new chisel or hammer. "You are an artisan, not a mere hewer of rock."

My tools were unloaded, and Boot led Nessie down to the stable. Starkey hefted one bag and I the other, and we followed John Good into a part of the house that was mostly finished.

The room was large and bare of furnishings, with five tall arching glass windows. Sun shone in but gave no warmth. "This will be the lesser hall," John Good said. "For feasts and celebrations. There will be a greater hall, big enough to hold five hundred people. But that wing of the house has not been started yet." He was clearly proud of his mansion, and some day it would indeed be very beautiful. But something more than pride swelled in his breast. He wanted me to tell him how wonderful it all was. He wanted me, like all his other workers, to praise him for all his great works. But I said not a thing.

"You've never seen the likes of this have you, Albion?" He stared, waiting for my obedient reply. "There is nothing as grand as this for a hundred miles." I was mum. I swore to myself I would not praise him, nor bow to him nor ask him for favor, like a servant.

"You're a quiet young man," he said at last. "Perhaps that is all for the best. You've come to work, not talk. And work you will."

I thought of the Reverend Mr. Yates and a sermon he'd preached just before I left Little Sion. His text was from Exodus, the first chapter, about the cruel slavery in which Pharaoh held the Hebrew people. "And he made their lives bitter with hard bondage, in stone and brick and all manner of labors in the making of great dwellings."

Now John Good is no Egyptian king, and I certainly am no Moses. But his lordly manner and hardness of heart might have matched the Pharaoh's.

He turned away and left, without a parting word.

Starkey led me down a long dark hallway and showed me the room where I would be sleeping. "We eat in the cellar," he said. "Don't be late, or you'll get nothing."

It is night now, and as I write, I hear no movement in the house. Compared to the hard, cold ground, this bed I sit on is quite fine. Starkey gave me a corn shuck mat to sleep on, and a lantern, and a good number of candles. My window is covered with boards, but I can pry them back and see a broad slice of the starlit sky. No moon tonight. And the comet is gone, back to where it came from, I suppose. I think of Watty and wish he were here.

September 25

A long day's labor. I saw John Good only briefly. Boot had taken me to the shed we'll use for the stoneshop, and I was rigging up a block and tackle for hoisting when he came in.

As on the day I first met John Good, when he invaded Mr. Bonness's stoneshop, he bore in close to me, as a preacher might to those uncertain folks sitting on a revival meeting's anxious bench. Tho he did not want repentance, I thought he desired of me a broken will. All the others here bow and sidle away at his approach, like slaves who've too many times felt the lash.

He is my employer and has promised goodly pay. I have contracted to provide my services for three months. Still, I will not call him my master.

He inspected my work, which at that point was merely preparations, and nodded his approval. "Start in on the blocks for the chimneys," he said. "I'll send two of the boys over to begin their learning with you."

The boys are men twice my age. They seem decent and agreeable, but quiet as dogs who've been whipped too much. I showed them how to work the hoist and gave them their first lesson in scoring and chipping.

One is called Willy. He bows his head and will not meet my eyes. The other, Chester, is tall and stoop-shouldered. They are slow of mind, I think, but with my supervision can be taught to do simple cutting.

We worked until dusktide and then a while longer with torches sconced on the beams. It is good to work at stone after my week away. The rhythm of the hammer is a comfort. The pinging noise, as steel hits steel, reminds me of Mr. Bonness and my home at Little Sion. The smell of rock dust in the air is a sweet perfume.

We worked longer than the others here. The carpenters laid their tools by at supper time. But it takes away the lonely feeling to lift the hammer and bring it down.

September 26

While we ate our dinner, I asked Willy and Chester where they'd come from. They both shrugged, as tho it didn't matter.

"Are your families hereabouts?"

Neither of them replied. I asked again, and Willy said quietly, "The Master says we don't talk about what's been, only what's to come."

Chester gravely nodded his agreement. "What's past is nothing. What's to come is all." He sounded like a schoolboy reciting his lesson.

They told me little more, only repeating the same sayings. The future is all; the past is nothing. We worked very hard today. Another apprentice has been given to me. Esra is a hulking boy who can hear, and obeys well, but who appears to be utterly dumb.

We worked the quarry a mile from Goodspell, cutting out some fine limestone blocks, and wagoned them back for Willy and Chester to hew.

September 28

No entry yesterday. Willy swung wild and hit my hand. The thumb is tender and already black-bruised. He's been moved off the stonecutting and sent back to hauling clay. Esra, who I assumed to be feeble-minded, is much sharper than I'd thought. He cannot speak, but does understand well. And he seems to enjoy the work. I told him I'd make him into a first-rate stonecutter, and he gave me back a big smile.

Must stop now. Thumb pains me severe.

September 30

I wasn't able to hold the chisel today. And seeing that Chester and Esra are doing well, I decided to wander the grounds. John Good must have a score of workers in his employ. There are carpenters and sawyers, shingle-makers and a smithy. Today I watched another section of roof being erected. The men scurry about the scaffolds like spiders on a web. It does my heart good to see the mansion house rising. And it much gratifies to know that my work will be part of this grand construction. But I wonder when my skills will be brought into play. Hewing chimney blocks and door sills is all well and good, but I long to return to finer carving.

I followed the track we'd come on, back through the little village of shanties and huts. A few women were here, boiling laundry in their big iron pots, tending gardens. Some looked up curious at me beneath their poke bonnets as I went by. But none spoke.

I'd gone a short distance down the trail, when I heard my name. There behind me was Boot. "No further," he said.

I asked what he meant.

"You are not allowed to go this far afield."

I kept walking, thinking this mere foolishness.

"Albion, listen to me," he commanded. "You cannot go home."

I explained I was merely taking a ramble, as my hand was little good for cutting today.

"You must return with me now. Mr. Good has given express instruction that you're not to leave the grounds."

I walked on. But he grabbed me by the arm and jerked me around to face him. "Now!" he said, anger turning his words black. "You must return with me now."

I might have outrun him. But Boot is a big man. And if I fled and he caught me up, I was afraid what punishment he'd mete out.

"Come with me," he growled. And so I did.

October 1

Pride is a poor teacher, and wrath a worse one. But still I was their pupil today. Ill-treated by Boot, as tho I were a small child, or a slave, I determined to sneak away from Goodspell, if only for a short space of time. All the while watching for Boot, I bade Esra and Chester to accompany me to the stable. We harnessed Nessie and took the wagon to the stone pit. I instructed them in their tasks: cut me blocks this length and this girth. Knowing it would take them much of the day to complete their tasks, I left them and went secret as a war-party scout down the ravine and then back up the other side.

I passed above the mill, staying well hidden. The rumble and whine faded. The tapping of hammers and the men's voices too receded, and I was soon swallowed in a sylvan green silence. Further I went, and met a trail that followed the path of a feeble little stream.

Then I began to ascend again. Goodspell is built in the lea of a great hill. We can never see the sun rise proper for the hill lies to our east. So I went up the trail, to find out what I might see from the top.

As I walked, it came to me that this was the first time I'd been truly alone since leaving Little Sion. No one shares my sleeping cell, but I know other workers are about. I hear voices at night, and footsteps in the hallway, and two nights ago what sounded like a tavern brawl: shouts and loud thumps and iron clanging on iron. But now, I thought, I was all by myself. No one could see me. No one in the world knew where I was. This was a lonesome feeling, but all the same a good one.

I miss the Bonness house mostly at night, when I lie on my pallet waiting for sleep. I miss my master's sure, steady instruction. And I miss Watty's distracted talk in the darkness. I wish I were back there, and the homesickness gnaws at me like a hungry worm.

But as I walked up the hill, my lonely feeling was not like that. There was a pleasurable part to it. I think the word is *melancholy.* I longed for something but didn't know what.

The trail grew steeper, winding this way and that. The afternoon sunshine only reached me in places, thin spears of light jabbing through the green canopy overhead.

Coming around a bend in the trail, I saw a rude little shanty built into the side of the hill. The walls were split logs and the roof shingled with broad strips of birch bark. No smoke came from the sticks-and-mud chimney. In a patch of sunlight only a rod or two wide was a meager little garden. Corn and beans and some pumpkins nigh onto orangey ripeness.

I stopped and listened. Far off in the woods, a crow was crying out to mark his territory. The echoes went all around, like a spectral bird dissolving into nothing as he flew. Then all was still. I was a fair hand at mimicking a crow's cry, and so to break the silence I called out to him.

"That won't do." A man's voice came from behind. I spun around, heart thumping into my throat like a two-pound hammer.

"You'll never fool her with such a poor measly cry."

The man was small, not even my height. He wore a tattered tow cloth shirt and leggings made of deerskin. Seen from afar, he might have been mistaken for a poor farmer's boy. But close up, and he approached me now, he was clearly no child. A week's worth of beard stubble and matted black hair obscured his face. His deep black eyes were not hidden tho. And when he spoke, his words were as deep as a bullfrog's groan.

"You can't fool the black bird with that wretched yelp," he said. "She's a keen one, boy. A right keen beastie."

I begged his pardon, as tho my feeble crow's cry were an insult.

"Don't mind, don't mind," he said. "Matters not." He walked around me, inspecting. He took hold of my shirt to feel the material. And then he sniffed at his fingers. "You work down at the big house. But you're not a carpenter's boy. Anybody with one eye can tell that. You're the stone mason."

I told him my name.

He nodded. "Have the other boys talked about the

old man on the hill?" he asked. "Do you hear the name Jack Smoke bandied about down there?"

"No, sir. No one says much. I ask and they sit mum as stones."

"Jack Smoke I am. Remember that name, boy. Remember Jack Smoke when it's all done."

"When what is done?"

"I was here before they came and I'll be here after they're gone. I'm Jack Smoke and this is my castle." He pointed to the shanty, grinning. "I'm the lord of all I survey."

"I was told that Mr. Good owns five thousand acres hereabouts."

"Depends on what you mean by 'owns.' John Good has some papers, and at the county courthouse those papers give a man what he wants. But Jack Smoke was here first, and he'll be here when it's all over."

"He allows you to stay here?"

This swelled up his anger, like a strong breath on coals. "Jack Smoke is here by no one's will but his own! I don't need permission to live on my own land." He pointed down the trail. "John Good came here and waved some papers, and now he has a quit claim to more land than any man should ever have. I'm not saying he stole it, but it didn't come into his hands fair nor right. I been here since I was a wee one, and I swear I'll be buried here. No land office jugglery can take a man's home away. Not if he's true."

I asked him if he lived alone.

"Jack Smoke is all the company that Jack Smoke needs." He puffed himself up with his words. "Jack Smoke owns this plot and he always will 'til the angel Gabriel blows the last trump. Jack Smoke is not afraid of land office papers and handfuls of gold money." Like a teakettle when it's moved away from the fire, his loud words and angry hand-waving ceased. "My ma lived here before me. A long while. Not just the first white woman, but the first white person, to stake her claim in the Genesee country. And my pa's people had a right to this place for longer than anybody can remember."

Then I understood. His black eyes and black hair were from his Indian blood. Tho the Seneca had been driven out long before I was born, there were still a few little enclaves scattered through York State. Some lived among the whites. And some, like Jack Smoke, hung on to their patches of land.

"You know what the word *birthright* means?" Before I could answer, he said, "Something they can't take away no matter what kind of deeds and lawyer-papers they got. This place is mine, by right of me being the last of my people."

He was silent a while, staring up toward the top of the hill. "The first and the last," he said, quiet as a mourner at a gravesite. "Jack Smoke is the last, and it was right here on the top of this hill where the first of his pa's people were borned." He took hold of my hands and squeezed. He's a small man, but strong as ironwood.

"Up there on the top is a cave where the great snake lived in the old, old days." He set off on a rambling story then, which I will not relate here in the order he told it. The gist of it was that a boy and girl took a snake as their pet and fed it continually until it was great and ever hungry. Soon all the tribe was set to hunting deer and wolf and panther to keep the great serpent from swallowing the people up. It grew so vast that they could not find enough game to ease its belly, and it then began to gorge on the people. At last only the boy and girl were left. They'd fled to the cave at the top of the hill. The snake followed them in, and by a clever trick, the children brought down a landslide and trapped the serpent inside. And these two children then became the parents of the new tribe.

By some confused turn in Jack Smoke's mind, the snake was killed or trapped forever, yet somehow too became the great Genesee River, winding and coiling all the way to Lake Ontario a hundred some miles north.

I wanted to know more, of course. Jack Smoke, however, had said his piece. "Maybe you come around another time and we'll talk again. But now you go back to where you come from."

October 2

As I ate breakfast today with the others, a boy came with a message. "The Master bids you come." I pointed out to him that I had not done eating yet, but he said, "Now. The Master wants you." I grabbed another johnnycake off the platter and drank the rest of my coffee in one gulp.

The boy led me through a part of the mansion house where I'd never been before. One short corridor was completely finished, with brass candle sconces and pretty flowered wallpaper. But turning a corner, we passed through a hallway that was still raw and undone. We went down steps and then up again. We went outside the building briefly, crossing a short stretch of mud by going gingerly across a split log. Then we were back inside again, climbing stairs. Behind a closed door, I heard a dog barking and growling. Then came a silent place, the wall-hangings and carpeted floor swallowing up every sound.

I was utterly lost, like Jonah wandering in the bowels of the whale. My guide went surely and without pause. It seemed we must have gone three times around the house before we arrived at John Good's chambers. "Go in. There," he said, pointing to a door studded with black iron nail heads.

He lifted the latch for me and gave me a slight shove. "Go in. He's waiting."

John Good sat at a great table, with papers and books and pots of ink strewn around him. He looked up from his work, like a wolf disturbed at its kill. But then his gaze softened. "Come here," he said. He opened a book and turned it to face me.

On one page was a beautiful engraving of a statue. It showed a woman with her hands clasped, raised to heaven in prayer. Her gown flowed around her like waves of water. Her face had great charm, but it was plain she felt not just joy, but joy intermixed with longing.

John Good turned the page and showed me another statue, of a small child with its head bowed. This too was wonderfully made: full of feeling and grace.

"I like these very much," John Good said. "They were fashioned by an artist of great skill. This book contains twenty-four plates such as these. I want you to take this back to your chamber and study them. And tomorrow you'll come here and tell me which of the statues you think best made."

Mr. Bonness has only three engravings of this quality. He let me see them now and again, to show me some element of sculptural technique. Then he put them back again, safely, in his chest of private treasures. And here I was, given an entire volume of such engravings and told to look them over and make a judgment as to their quality.

"I can't say one is better. I have no right to judge a master's work," I said.

"All I want you to do, Albion, is to tell me which one you like best. Which one suits your fancy." He gestured as one would shoo away a fly. "Go. Do as I've told you. Spend a few hours in the stoneshop overseeing Esra and Chester. But today your most important task is to con these pages closely. We'll speak again tomorrow."

I left, and my guide led me to my room. The entire trip back I held the book close to my chest. It weighed much, and I was afraid to drop such a precious volume. It has great value, I'm sure, in the marketplace of dollars and shillings and pence. But it is precious to me for another reason.

I write now with the volume open before me, and I study the plates, one by one.

October 3

I am up early this morn, before the sun. John Good's book lies before me, and I am resolved to capture the pictures in a web of words. I will need to return the book, and I want very much to remember the engravings. I'll want, I'm sure, descriptions to jog my memory some day.

I have removed the boards from my window, and the dawn light is now streaming through onto the book. Such a delight. Such a gift.

The engraving before me shows a young woman in an attitude of somber reflection. Her head is bowed, and her hair falls around her like a liquid veil. Tho she is carved in stone, the artisan shows such skill that it seems her hands tremble with emotion.

Turning the book leaf I see a singularly affecting picture. This is called "Acteon pursued by the Hounds of Diana." The hapless hunter runs from his pursuers, and already horns have begun to sprout on his head. Such a look of terror in his eyes! Gazing at the engraving, I can feel, too, the panting of the terrible dogs and hear their wild baying voices.

On the next page are a pair of young children crouched in prayer. The sculptor has fashioned them in a most pleasing way, with a smoothness and grace of form that charms my eye. The engraving puts me in mind of

Watty. The children seem to wait, expectant of some miracle. There is longing in their faces, yet also assurance. They wear the same expressions as Watty when he told me of the far-off trumpet.

I have set the quill down a moment and read over my first three entries. It is clear that I will never truly capture the engravings in words. I wonder if another, reading these words, could see what I see. And what must the statues themselves be like, if the engravings of them conjure up such wonderful feelings in me? I would so much like to see even one of these works with mine own eyes.

Tho words are meager and weak to hold the images, I will continue. The next I pondered over for a very long time. It is called "Amphitrite Ravished by Poseidon." The engraving shows a young goddess or nymph, unclothed, writhing and twisting. Behind her, but largely unseen in this picture, is Poseidon, who I believe was a heathen god of the sea. At their feet water splashes in marble waves. The two bodies are twined and tangled in a way that causes me great uneasiness to contemplate. I can see only a portion of his aspect behind the girl: a great grizzled beard and one mad eye.

I look at the picture, then go to the next, yet come

back again. Three times I moved on and turned the page, and three times I have returned to gaze at the pale white girl struggling. Her form is graceful, smooth, and sleek. Hers is no angelic grace, however, but another kind.

I have put down my quill a moment and closed my eyes. John Good has instructed me to choose the engraving I fancy to be the best. But how should I answer that question? If I return again and again does that mean that the picture of Amphitrite is my favorite? Or is there another reason I cannot move on to the next page? Surely other sculptures in the book are of just as high an artistic quality. Still, I come back and gaze at the girl. At first I thought her expression to be simple terror. A great and awful sovereign has seized her. She fights to free herself. But looking deeper into her face, looking a long while, I can see it's not just fear but some other power of feeling that consumes her. I want to know what that feeling is, but I am also afraid to know.

October 3 later (night)

I gave up trying to catalog the marvelous engravings and simply pored over them. I laid down my quill, and when the ink was dry I closed my journal book and went page after page through the volume.

The boy came to my door and told me to accompany him again to John Good's apartments. We went a different route, I think, through the half-built mansion. Again it was up here and down there, around and over and back. Yesterday I thought the house to be an infinite maze of corridors and halls and chambers. But today it occurred to me that the boy might be going a crazy route to confuse me or keep me from finding his master's chambers.

We passed through one room where carpenters were laying down floor boards. They were not yet half done, so we had to go careful as circus rope walkers across the floor beams. Below was a large room that appeared to be mined entirely into the bedrock. All four walls were raw limestone, badly cut and dressed. Holding the book against my chest, my balance was poor. I tottered, looking down into the stony pit. But the boy took ahold of me by the shoulder and led me across to safety.

Again we came to the great oaken door, and I was told to go inside.

Again John Good looked up from his sheafs and drifts of papers. "Come here," he said. "You've brought the book. Lay it here and show me which work you like best."

As I approached he cleared a place on the table. "Here," he said, thumping his finger on the scarred black wood. I put the book down and turned the pages. But I stopped before showing him my favorite. I asked him why he had wanted me to examine the engravings.

"You're a stonecutter, are you not? You've made angels. I saw that in your master's shop at Little Sion. You're a young man of unusual ability, but little experience." I owned that this was true, but still did not understand his reasoning.

"I've brought you here to fashion a great work. You've begun your lesser task: to superintend the cutting of crude blocks. And in that you've succeeded admirably. However, I did not hunt across the width of York State to find a simple stone-hewer. I was searching for one such as you." He fixed me with his ice-water eyes. "You are the chosen one."

For a reason I don't truly understand, I thought of Watty then. I thought of him looking up at the comet, and listening to the sky, and whispering his strange and cryptic sayings.

"Albion!" John Good said, like a schoolmaster calling a dreamy scholar back to attention. "Have you heard what I've said?" Indeed, John Good was still speaking while my mind flew back to Watty and Little Sion.

I told him no, I wasn't listening.

"Attend, Albion," he boomed. "Attend with all your senses."

He reached into a leathern bag and drew forth a small piece of whitish-yellow stone. On one side it was raw, having been broken from its bed. But the rest was smooth and rounded like ice that forms at a waterfall. He handed me the stone and asked me to examine it.

The surface was pleasant to the touch and the color pleasing to the eye.

"Can you cut an image in that stone?"

"It's far too small."

"No. You misunderstand. Could you work in this type of stone? A much larger piece?"

It had a fine grain and, from my initial examination, it seemed soft enough that my tools could shape it. It might have been limestone somehow liquefied and then made hard again, like the drips of water that freeze and melt on a sunny winter's day.

I told him this, and he nodded his approval. "Then let us return to the engravings," he said, flipping the pages of the book.

But I was tired of confusion, tired of half-truths and evasions. "You must tell me, and tell me now, why you've brought me here."

He looked up, startled by the heat of my voice. "You must learn to bridle your tongue, boy. Others in a loftier position than you have lived to regret such insolence. Have a care, or you'll find yourself in as sorry a state as Esra or Chester."

Still I would not back down. "Tell me why I am here."

"All in good time," he said, flipping the pages of the book.

"No! You will tell me now or I gather my belongings

and leave." I knew that finding my way back to Little Sion alone was nearly impossible. I'd wander forever, lost. Or I'd starve. But I was determined to go if John Good didn't explain all to me right then. "I will tarry no longer if you continue to evade my questions. I am a free man."

There was a long silence while we both contemplated what I'd said. Never in my life had I declared that I was a man. Just fourteen years old, alone and unsure, but I had said it. And I said it again. "I am a free man."

"And so you are," he agreed. "Very well. Listen and I will explain."

He hefted the piece of smooth pretty stone. "There is a cave on the hill above Goodspell. This stone comes from there. My wife, whom I loved more than anything in this world, lies there. It is her tomb, but yet a crude and unfinished place of rest. You will begin tomorrow to carve the stone there as a monument to her. I hunted for months to find an artisan who could do her justice, who could fashion a memorial that will express my love and my loss."

He turned the book to face me. The engraving showed a woman crouched at a broken stone altar. She was bowed down, heavy with grief. But she was beautiful, too. Her suffering had made her more so. “Hence the engravings. I have been poring over these since my wife died, trying to find an image that will tell of my loss. And also tell of her divine excellence.”

He dug his hands into a sheaf of papers and then dropped them to the table top as tho they were dead autumn leaves. “I have struggled to design a monument for her. I have sat here day in and out scrawling with pencil. I have spent much money on books such as the one I gave you last night, hoping to find an image that would capture my grief exactly. But that task now falls to you, Albion. Use your artistry in tribute to my wife, and I will reward you handsomely.”

Again he asked me which engraving in the book I liked best. He told me the truth today, and so I did likewise. Without hesitation, without shame, I turned the pages back and said, “This one.” It was the image of Amphitrite, ravished by Poseidon. More so than yesterday, she was beautiful to me. But it was not mere beauty that held my attention. She was filled with a feeling I could only guess at. Her heart quaked with fear, but also a bewildered longing.

There came a knock on the door. Before John Good could say "Enter," the door swung open and in came a girl. We were silent a moment, as she regarded me. "This is the new boy?" she asked. She is my age, or perhaps a year or two older. However, she carries herself with the air of a grown woman. The way she said the word *boy* stung me.

I looked away from her, and my gaze settled again on the engraving of Amphitrite. Such a raw outpouring of feeling there: terror, and something else, something akin to a powerful joy. Then I looked back at the girl. Her eyes were fixed on me, probing, it felt, to see inside my heart. Either way I looked, I recoiled. The girl, lovely, but haughty as a queen, surveyed me with her fierce stare. And Amphitrite struggled on the page, as if imploring me for aid.

I wanted to flee the room, flee Goodspell forever. I wanted to be back at Little Sion, safe in my workshop. I wanted to feel Mr. Bonness's sure hand and hear his calm and steady voice.

"Is this the new boy?" she said again, louder, impatient with our silence.

"I am Albion Straight, journeyman stonecutter."

John Good added, "He's here to work on the monument."

A look of unmistakable scorn darkened the girl's pretty face. "You've brought a boy here for such an important task?" She came closer, and walked around me, a full circuit, like a fickle buyer inspecting a new horse.

"He has done excellent work," John Good said. "I have seen the efforts of his craft and he is certainly equal to the task." The way he spoke was almost apologetic. For the master of such an estate, for a man of wealth and power, he seemed rather weak in the girl's presence. "Albion's skill is remarkable. There is an angel in his master's shop —"

But the girl cut him off with a wave of her hand. "He's a boy. He can't be any older than I."

John Good turned to me, embarrassed by the girl's contempt. "I should introduce you. Albion, this is Michal. She will be the model for your work. My hope, my desire, is for you to fashion a memorial with a central female figure. And I want her to have Michal's face and form."

The girl met my gaze, as if challenging me to argue.

A glimmer of a smile came and went. But how to understand that smile? The sneer of a fine lady or a hint of welcome?

"Boot will take you up to the cave tomorrow. I want you to examine the form of the stone there and tell me where best the memorial shall be cut. You will have assistance if you need it, men to haul out the rubble, carpenters to build a scaffold if you think that is necessary. When you have the groundwork completed, Michal will join you and I want a statue like the ones in the book carved to the memory of my dear wife."

The girl gave a shake of her auburn locks and said, "I hope your skill is as great as my father claims. He is not a man whom it is wise to disappoint." And with that, she left the room.

"Michal is your daughter?" I asked, quiet as the sole worshiper in a vast church.

"Yes, she is my daughter and the image of her mother. If you can capture her in stone, I shall be a very happy man." He pushed two more volumes across the table toward me. "Study these engravings. There are tombs depicted here from cathedrals and cemeteries throughout Europe. Study them and tell me tomorrow which design you think best."

October 4

I spent much of last night with the books. A boy brought me two dozen candles for my lantern and pencils and a goodly sheaf of paper to work on. The noises within the mansion house dwindled as I worked, until it was silent. Still I examined the engravings, one by one, read the descriptions, and made notes that I shall show to John Good. Such a horde of treasure these volumes are! Each page is a delight and yet also a reproof. How can I create anything that might satisfy John Good when he's seen these masterpieces? The sculptors represented here were men with decades of experience, with all the treasures of Greece and Rome to examine and learn from. I am a boy, and I have seen nothing more than a few grave markers. I am sore afraid that John Good thinks too highly of my skills.

October 4 (later)

Boot took me up to the cave, and now my doubts grow worse.

It is a vast place, beautiful and strange. My heart quails at the thought of spending weeks or even months inside.

We followed the trail that I'd gone on a few days back and passed near Jack Smoke's shanty. I looked over that way as we went and Boot said, "Stay clear of the half-breed. He's not one to meddle with. If he comes around while you're up at the cave, don't talk or even look him in the eye. If he persists, tell me or one of the others and we'll stake a guard. He's a wicked one with the knife. Some of the workers have tangled with him and gotten the worse for it. Jimmie Conn is missing two fingers and Bart Smith has a scar as long and vicious as a rattlesnake on his leg."

As the trail rose, I caught glimpses of the landscape beyond Goodspell. Much of the forest was still uncut here. And the hills were much steeper than those around

Little Sion. Here and there I could see raw rock jutting out through the green. And there, almost to the horizon, was a flash of silvery-green that I took for the Genesee. "Is that the river?" I asked Boot.

He paused and followed the line of my sight. "Couldn't say. Mayhaps it is."

We kept climbing. Near the summit a black mouth yawned in the side of the hill. Around were black-speckled boulders and a few piles of broken stone, the result, I reckoned, of some earlier attempts at mining. There was a rough log hut built at the cave mouth with a pile of firewood nearby.

Boot pointed to the hut. "You can store your tools and sundries in there. Mr. Good has instructed the kitchen wenches to bring you up a dinner every day."

But I cared little about the shanty. My mind was fixed on the cave mouth and what lay inside.

Boot went to the hut and brought back two lanterns and a half dozen candles. He unfolded the handful of cabbage leaves he'd carried up from the mansion house and blew on the hot coals they'd sheltered. Soon he had them glowing red again and held one of the candlewicks close. With some soft curses and puffing, he had the candles burning and placed three inside each lantern.

"There's your place," he said, pointing to the cave's mouth. It seemed a strange way to talk, as if I were a dog and he was saying, "There's your kennel."

We entered, pushing back the shadows with our lanterns. The first chamber was twisty and gnarled, barely wide enough for us to pass through. But the next opened wide to the sides and above, larger than the church sanctuary in Little Sion. Our lanterns' light barely reached the walls. And the ceiling loomed thick with darkness.

"This is what the Master calls the Great Hall. Here's where he wants the statues made." Boot said this plain and simple. But my heart grew weak at this prospect. I could barely conceive what my labors would be. I certainly had no hope that I could fashion this vast cave into a memorial to a beloved wife. The largest stone I'd ever cut was not even as tall as I, and this cave reached beyond my sight.

And it troubled me to think of working for weeks or months in the same place where the body was interred. Boot explained that his master's wife was laid to rest here in a small chamber off the Great Hall.

I wanted to sink down right there and never rise. I wondered why I, of all the boys I knew, had been chosen for apprenticeship to Mr. Bonness. Wherefore was I singled out for this awful task? I thought of my brothers, who'd never seen a stonecutter's chisel. Right now they were in the fields harvesting. It was endless and backbreaking work, but it was in the sun's light, not hidden inside a cave. I pictured the wheat fields and the bright edge of the scythe flashing in the sun. And then I peered around me at this dismal place and I wanted to weep.

"Am I a prisoner then?" I asked.

Boot didn't understand my question.

"Am I to spend my days here in the darkness? Every day with only candles to light my way?"

"The Master tells everyone that you have great skills. No one else can transform this cave into a place of beauty."

We were silent a long while, listening to water dripping far off in the shadows like tears. I thought then: I've been stolen from my home and now I'm to be buried alive in his vast damp hole in the earth.

Boot held his lantern out in a different direction. There on the wall were growths of wet rock, like bulbous roots. Their color was a reddish gold. Their surface was wrinkled and twisted. Both beautiful and ugly at the same time, they hung in strange array.

We moved on, deeper into the cavern. Here great spears of white stone hung down like icicles. In places, others jutted up directly below these spears, like reflections in the surface of a pond. Still deeper in the cave, we saw places where columns of stone reached from the roof, high above, to the floor of the cave. Our lantern light flickered, and I felt a slight wind. Somewhere high in the darkness, a crack led all the way to the surface.

Just then we heard a low groaning, as from an immense distance away. Boot was afraid, but hid his fear with a sour expression, and by saying, "Some fools believe this cave leads all the way to hell. I've heard tell that the Black One himself can be seen flying out from the cave-mouth." He sneered at such talk, but when we heard the noise again, he ushered me back the way we'd come.

The noise came then as a rumble, like an enormous millstone turning. Perhaps it was wind trapped in the bowels of the cave, but to me it sounded like a rough scaly form sliding over rock. I thought of the story Jack Smoke had told me, of the vast serpent the Indian children had imprisoned there. And I did not linger as Boot hurried me toward daylight.

Outside at last, I breathed deeply, basking in the bright sun's warmth. How delightful the trees looked, how comforting the sight of clouds and the sound of birds were to me then. What a burden I carried inside the cave, as tho the entire mountain's mass were weighing down on my shoulders.

October 5

I have met again with John Good, and told him that I cannot fulfill the task he's set for me. He was implacable, insistent, unyielding. He told me I would not return to Little Sion until I'd done the work he'd engaged me for.

October 6

Another meeting with John Good, whose face I've grown to hate. Again he told me plainly that I must set to work in the cavern. He told me to start first with plans. He gave me more books to study over and commanded that I bring him a sketch for the memorial. I took the books, and they lie before me now in my cell. But the task is impossible.

October 7

John Good has called for me. I refused to go. Boot has come twice to my cell and demanded I follow him. But I will not go. This journal seems now a hateful thing, a mere record of my despair.

October 8

John Good has relented somewhat. He has agreed to let me first carve a likeness out of free-standing stone, in a large room he has arranged as a kind of studio or shop. It is in the other wing of the mansion house, with windows that face north for the best light.

Tho my desire is to be gone from this loathsome place, it seems wise for me now to submit. Better to be a prisoner in the mansion house, where I can see the sun and the sky, than in the cave.

I have agreed to work in the studio, and today I met with Michal again. She came with her governess, a Mrs. Strand, who glowers and stares like a surly watchdog. She is shaped like a mastiff, too, with a broad forehead and a mouth that seems to contain too many teeth. Clearly distrusting me, she sniffs and growls as she watches me work.

John Good has had a large piece of limestone brought into the studio, and I will begin with that. I've instructed the carpenters to build a frame or simple pedestal to hold the stone. And a wooden platform also where Michal will pose.

She stands a few yards away, haughty and proud, but her words are no longer so full of venom. She is indeed a lovely girl, and if I might capture even a hint of her beauty in the stone, then I shall be satisfied. Her dress is of white muslin, very fine and pretty, and cinched up high above her waist. Her hair is unbound, coiling red-brown tresses which reach below her shoulders.

"What are you writing?" she asks.

"Notes," I say, and keep on recording my observations. Unless John Good has told her about it, she does not know about my journal. I'm sure it would infuriate her to know I was recording my observations. Or again, perhaps it would be flattering to know I have so much to say about her.

"What kind of notes?"

I ignore her question.

"Albion!" she says, and I look up to meet her angry eyes. This is, I believe, the first time she's said my name. "Tell me what you're writing there."

"Before I begin such an important undertaking, I need to have my thoughts in order. I am required to fashion a memorial that speaks of both sadness and beauty. I cannot begin by merely smashing at the stone."

This seems to satisfy her, but in truth I have no plan, no idea of how to proceed, indeed no hope.

October 8 (later)

She agreed to stand one hour for me. I suspect it plucks at her vanity that John Good would want her form made immortal in stone. I also suspect that it gives her some pleasure to be around me. At one point she told Mrs. Strand to go and fetch her other slippers, and while we were alone together I fancy her expression softened some.

But this is mere diversion. One hour with Michal and the rest of the day in despair. I did as I agreed, examining all the books. And I here mark down those engravings which I think best express the pain and loss which John Good must feel:

PAGE 11: Grave memorial of Princess Caroline of Utrecht. (Note: Where is Utrecht? I shall inquire). This grave monument is my favorite of all those in the book. Some are far more ornate, with winged creatures and pillars and fiery crowns. But this memorial has a plain stark beauty, showing the princess lying in state on top of a coffin-like platform. A pair of flowers (lilies?) droops from her hands, which are folded over her breast.

PAGE 18: Grave marker for a Joshua FitzWilliam. In this engraving the figure stands upright. It does not depict the man whose tomb this is, but instead is a female form, symbolic, I suppose, of general mourning. Flowing robes and hair, a languid stone garland, a kind of liquid grace. In the engraving it appears she is weeping. I have seen memorials discolored this way: stained by the passing of time as tho cold stone faces could weep real tears.

PAGE 27: Not a design I would think useful to copy. But there is one detail which I find myself repeatedly drawn back to: the little face or soul effigy rising as if it were from the ground. Overhead is the angel Gabriel with his trumpet, and he is blasting the last clarion call for the dead. He is well fashioned, but unremarkable. It is the tiny round head or face rising below which draws my attention. I cannot say for certain why.

October 9 (early)

The first snow of the year. Only a small amount that melted with the rise of the sun, but still it augers an early winter. Once the snow comes in earnest, my hopes of returning to Little Sion grow dimmer. I prayed this morning for courage and now must pack up my journal and ink and books and go to face John Good.

October 9 (dusk)

A long and harrowing day. First I went with my young guide on our roundabout path to John Good's apartments. Thus far we've never gone the same way twice. At times it seems that the mansion house contains an infinite number of rooms and corridors.

For the first time, I wondered where Michal's chambers might be found. Surely she lives here, inside the mansion house. But it seems most passing odd that I've never once encountered her going here or there in the house.

I laid the book of engravings on John Good's study table. He nodded gravely, as tho I'd returned from some great quest with a treasure. He asked which funeral monuments I thought best.

I began by telling him that all were well beyond my ability. "I am a boy, not a master carver. I have only wielded the hammer and chisel for three years. There is no way that I might fashion such beautiful creations."

He brushed this objection away as tho it were a piece of dust. "I saw the angel you carved in Charles Bonness's shop. I am convinced of your ability." And with that he asked me again which design I held in highest esteem.

I consulted this, my journal, and showed him the three designs I thought best.

He concurred. "You have the skill with hammer and you have the eye needed to see the fitting beauty. Now I want you to draw me a design. At this point, it need not be complete nor detailed. But I want, also, to see what is in your mind's eye."

This seemed an added burden. For I might have the stonecutter's skill, but I am no draughtsman with pen and ink. I told him so.

"They can be just sketches at this point. I'll expect to see them tomorrow." With that I was dismissed. But I did not leave the chamber just yet.

"You have a question?"

"Yes," I said. "When will I be allowed to go home?"

"You've barely begun." These words were as leaden-heavy as the tolling of a church bell for a funeral meeting. "You've just begun," he said again. "Now, go and get to work. Carve me an image of my Michal. Make her as beautiful as the angel I saw."

The boy tugged at my sleeve, insistent. "I'll show you the way," he whispered.

"No!" The strength of my voice surprised both John Good and myself. "I must have assurance that I'll be released in a timely manner. When can I go home?"

"When you've fulfilled your obligation to me. And the sooner you set to work the sooner you will have completed your tasks."

The boy took me by the hand and led me to the door. We went up and down and around and found ourselves at last at the stonecutting room. Through the window, I could see that all the snow was gone. The small pond down the north slope lay steaming in the bright sunlight.

Michal was waiting for me. Her impatient anger melted quickly as I set out paper and pencils. I thought of all the engravings that I'd studied this week. I tried to picture Michal in all the postures. Surely what I should conjure in stone is grief, dire mourning. But something of hope too. And perhaps something beyond that. If I can color her expression with some of the longing that Amphitrite felt, a hint of the fear and rapture, then perhaps my work will suffice.

I had her pose this way and that, making rough sketches of each. I imagine that Michal would do well on the theatrical stage. She seems to like to play make-believe and even more to have the gaze of others fixed on her. I began to wonder if the first day we met she was merely playing a role: the haughty princess to my lowly artisan. Perhaps all her proud and lofty ways were merely a performance.

I don't know what to believe any longer. Everything about Goodspell seems tainted with untruth. I was lied to by William Williams; it was his trickery which brought me here. John Good told me first he wanted my services for simple stonecutting, and now I am to spend months in a dismal cave making a grave memorial. Michal appeared to hold me in contempt. However, today she hangs on to my every word.

But I have made my decision: the only way to leave this place is to fulfill my obligation. I will set to work in earnest. I will carve a beautiful angel for John Good in memory of his late wife. Then I will take my pay and return home.

The odious Mrs. Strand looms too near as I work. I ask her to take a place farther away. With a snort, she moves her chair a few feet back and resumes her knitting. Her distrust of me appears to be complete. It seems she thinks I've been to Europe (fond wish!) and studied the great sculptures there. She fears I will fashion an indecent likeness of Michal. It is true that many of the great works I've studied in John Good's books show the figures unclothed. And tho I've made it clear that this is hardly my intention, still she watches me with suspicion and even fear.

Michal struck a pose which she had seen in one of the books, but it seems false, empty of true feeling. I asked her to raise this hand, lower that. I told her to let her head droop, bend the knee, turn and turn back. But no posture was fitting.

October 10

Again I have met with Michal, and as I write these words, she is standing on the little wooden platform in a posture of abject grief. I drew a sketch in pencil to show John Good, but I think it better to capture her in words than in pencil lines.

Her head is lifted slightly, as tho she searches a far-off horizon for some sign of hope. Her shoulders droop, her hands loosely hold a garland of little paper flowers. Her form is more relaxed than before, as tho weary with mourning. But it is the expression on her face which I hope to capture in stone: one of infinite sadness.

Why so much gaiety and teasing yesterday (she called me "Master Albion") and today such quiet grief? Why this heavy silence?

October 10 (later)

The previous entry was interrupted by the sudden appearance of John Good. He entered without knocking, and Mrs. Strand stood like the dutiful (and I would say fearful) servant. Michal's posture and expression changed too: from grieving to alarm.

"I've come to observe your progress," John Good declared, like a schoolmaster who suspects his pupils of mischief.

I showed him my pencil sketches, and he pronounced them acceptable. "Set to work then. Set to work. I want to hear the clang of your hammer." He had not even acknowledged Michal's presence yet. "Leave us," he said brusquely. "I need to speak with Mr. Straight."

Mrs. Strand quickly gathered up her skeins and needles and ushered Michal out of the room.

John Good grunted with relief once the door was shut. "She's given you no trouble then?"

I told him I didn't understand his question.

"Michal — she has been cooperative? She does as she is told?"

I didn't know how to answer him. I am a virtual captive in this house, not one to give orders and expect obedience.

John Good sat down with a loud sigh. "She has ever been a vexation to me," he said quietly. "I fear that I was entirely too lax in her upbringing. And the result has been a girl who shows little respect and less love for her father." This aspect of John Good I had never seen before. He seemed to want my sympathy. "Indeed, Michal is unruly, rebellious, ungovernable. Last night we quarreled, and I was forced to use rather severe punishment. I am loath to do such a thing. Truly, it grieves me sorely to punish her. But what am I do to?"

Why was he telling me this? I wondered. Why disburden himself in this manner?

"You will fashion a beautiful angel for me, won't you?" he asked.

"That is my hope and my intent."

"You must study Michal's face closely, Albion. Study her and make her live in the stone. Bring her back to me." His words were baffling, but the feeling that gave them life was clear. John Good's mourning was deep and sincere.

"She was beautiful," he whispered. "She was my life." By this, I took him to mean his wife. "And when she died I was bereft. You can't understand this, Albion. To be robbed of such a treasure. All that remained to me was our little girl, Michal. Her mother died bringing her into the world. The two of them lived only a day together. My wife was feverish, hardly able to speak. But she held Michal for a day and then she passed. And all I had to remember her by was our tiny babe." He was quiet a while, considering.

"When she was little, I could not bring myself to punish her. Every cry, every tear, wounded me. She learned well how to make me feel remorse for my wrath. But now I must discipline her. I could overlook the little wrongs of a toddling babe. However, her misdeeds are of a far more serious nature now. She must be chastened. She must be reined in like a wild horse."

Shaking off this mood, he told me to hand him my sketches so he could look at them more carefully. "Yes, this will do. This will do well. You can bring her back to me, in stone if not in the flesh." He studied the pages a while longer.

"I've waited fifteen years to build her memorial because I needed a model, a living image of her. And now Michal is of age. Her appearance is exactly that of her mother, as she was when I first met her. I look at Michal and I see her mother. There were other reasons to wait on the memorial. My business waxed profitable. I gathered a fortune and bought the land and brought together my craftsmen and laborers. But all of this would have been for naught if we had no living image to work from. Michal has reached the age, the perfect age."

He got up and grasped my hands. "You must capture her face perfectly. You must make her live again."

I told him I would do my best.

"Your best, your best," he whispered. "Your best must be perfect."

October 11

Today I began the statue. With great uneasiness, I placed a point chisel against the block and brought my hammer down on it. The sound startled Michal. We'd spent a while getting her into position, studying my sketches and talking about the feeling that must animate her expression. And with one hammer-stroke, it was all gone. She jerked as tho the hammer had hit her and not the chisel's head. To me the sound is like a beautiful chime. To her, it seemed, it was a musket ball exploding against a fortress wall.

But she resumed her role again, conjuring the feeling back and holding her arms just so. I placed the chisel at a steep angle to the stone and took another swing. She winced but maintained her pose. And so we began.

Mr. Bonness had taught me the stonecutter's three-tap rhythm. It feels reassuring to be back at something I know. Tap tap tap — pause — tap tap tap. I look over at my model, then at the sketches which John Good approved, and move back into the rhythm. Chips of stone fall to the floor. The familiar sweet dusty smell reaches my nostrils. I am, as long as the hammer swings, at peace.

October 12

Another day at work. Michal now is comfortable with the sound of the hammer. Because it is loud, and because I must concentrate, there's little time for us to talk. Still, there are brief pauses, as I brush off the surface or consider the lines in the stone. She asks a question now and then. "What do you call that tool?" or "Why do you keep switching hammers?" But once, today, she inquired not of my efforts but of me.

"How did you learn this art?" Michal said. Mrs. Strand glared over at me, as tho demanding I remain mum.

"I was apprenticed to Mr. Bonness. It was pure happenstance. I had no calling, no interest, no experience. My father agreed to this arrangement. I think he was relieved to have me out from under his care. I was never much use on the farm. My brothers could cut hay or walk behind the plow from dawn until dusk, but my fancy would wander. The scythe might cease its swinging or the furrows grow more meandering. My father thought I'd never be any use on the farm."

Mrs. Strand got up from her chair and cleared her throat with much vigor. But I ignored the hateful old woman. It was clear to me that she had no power over us, only the ability to annoy.

I looked directly at her and continued, "I traveled to

Little Sion at the age of eleven and have not seen my family since that date."

Michal asked if this did not grieve me. And I told her, "No, but I miss my master dearly. And his boy, Watty, who has been a true friend to me." Indeed, I thought, there are times I feel him with me as a comfort. Tho far in flesh, he is near in spirit.

Returning to the work, I picked up a heavier punch chisel and brought the hammer down a little harder than I should. Thankfully, I did no real damage to my work, but the gesture scared Mrs. Strand back to her place.

October 13

After consulting the sketches, I spent a while drawing on the stone with charcoal sticks. The head and upper body were emerging from the rough stone. At this point, there was no practical reason for Michal to wear the exact expression we desired. It would be a long while before I could begin to shape her eyes and lips and ears. But it would help, I thought, to keep that look of sadness ever before me.

At times I think of Michal as a kind of specter. She can be so quiet, so motionless. And when she walks, there's a ghostly grace to her tread. And when I look at my work, it seems that her form comes forth from the stone like an apparition: white and indistinct.

Michal abhors the old woman's presence more than I. Today she instructed Mrs. Strand to go back to their chambers and fetch a certain book. She claimed that she wanted her governess to read to her as I worked. So (happy event!) we were not vexed by Mrs. Strand for a goodly space of time.

"I do so loathe this place," Michal said, as soon as we heard the footsteps fade. "I hate it with all of my heart." I wondered if that were the root out of which all her haughtiness and wrath grew. "I want to leave. But when I tell my father that, his face waxes black with anger. 'This is our home!' he shouts at me. 'Here we will stay forever.' But if that were true, if I could look into the future and see that I shall never leave, then I think I should throw myself into a well to drown."

I continued to work. My attention, however, was no longer on the contours of the stone, but on the story she told.

"Do you know why I am the model for this statue?" she said. "I am, he swears, the perfect image of my mother. I don't believe that, tho. She's been gone for as long as I've been alive. He has no drawing nor painting of her. How could he keep that image alive in his fancy for fifteen years? I think he has forgotten what my mother looked like and has replaced her visage with mine." She slumped, as tho the heavy burden she'd been carrying finally grew too much to bear.

She went to Mrs. Strand's chair and sat. "I've heard you complain to my father that he treats you less like a craftsman than a prisoner. But I am the true prisoner here, Albion. I will never be allowed to leave. He buys me wonderful gifts from far away, thinking it will ease my longing to escape. But these trinkets just serve to make my desire even stronger. This house will someday be beautiful. He has promised me gardens and parks and ponds and glades. No matter how charming, however, if I might not leave, it is still a prison."

Then we heard the hurried clump of Mrs. Strand's

approach. Michal quickly got up from the chair and resumed her pose. I went back to my work, tho my hands were weaker now, I think, and my eye less keen.

October 15

No entry yesterday: much work, little talk. Mrs. Strand looms like a gorgon over us. We must find a way to be free of her presence.

October 16

Michal's face begins to emerge, and her shoulders. I think with every stroke of the the hammer, every bit of stone that falls, a tiny portion of Michal's haughtiness too falls away. She is afflicted sorely with a loneliness that I may only glimpse, but not truly comprehend. She told me that her father has ever been her closest companion. But what kind of companionship that must be! "He wants me always with him. He wants me, day or night, at his beck and call."

John Good came today to examine the progress of my work. As tho his presence were something too terrible to be born, Mrs. Strand fled to the outer corridor.

He walked a compass all the way around the statue three times, nodding. He reached out once to touch the form, but drew his hand back, as tho the stone were white-hot fire and might give him unbearable pain. "Yes, I have made the right decision. This work will be a fitting tribute to Michal," he said.

She winced, hearing this. I was perplexed by his comment. For wasn't the statue to be in memory of his wife? It wasn't until then that I understood. Both mother and daughter bore the same name.

"Father," Michal said, "I know you want Albion to make haste. I know how much you desire to see the statue done." Her voice was different now, with a note of wheedling or coaxing in it. "Albion will not say this, for fear of offense, but it is plain that the presence of Mrs. Strand slows his progress. Her coughing and sighing and murmuring are a distraction. And she fidgets so, up and down, pestering with her comments."

He told Michal that he'd speak with Mrs. Strand about the problem.

"No, father, she can't be here any longer. As you can see, Albion's work will soon require a delicacy of touch, concentration, that her presence will destroy."

Again John Good said he'd instruct Mrs. Strand to be less of a bother.

"That won't do. She cannot be in the room with us." I'd seen father and daughter so little together that this interview came as a surprise. She wheedled and he refused. She pleaded and smiled and he weakened. She pouted silent a moment and he looked away.

"Father, you've told me this is the most crucial aspect of Goodspell. Remember: 'All the turrets and halls and parks and great chambers will mean nothing without a fitting memorial.' You've found the artisan to make a perfect monument. But he must work undisturbed."

They haggled like two peddlers, and in the end Michal won. I was fascinated to observe them bargain. For all Michal's talk of being a prisoner, she wields great power over John Good. They both have their realms of influence, and each is careful not to trespass on the other's. I understand better now what John Good meant when he told me that it grieved him to punish Michal. He clearly loved her deeply. She is indeed the only thing in this world that he loves. To inflict suffering or greater sadness on her must vex him sorely.

October 17

I write now in the studio room. Michal sits in the chair which Mrs. Strand had occupied. The old woman is in the outer corridor. But we will not be, John Good has promised, annoyed or distracted by her presence.

I worked a goodly while this morning, and we now take an interval for rest. Michal had used all her wiles on John Good to liberate us from her governess, but there was truth in what she had said. I am able to work more easily without the perpetual noises and movements of the old woman.

Michal, too, is changed. She speaks more freely to me. From her conversation, I understand now where John Good's wealth had come from. "When I was a wee little one we lived in the great city of New York. And my father traded in all kinds of valuable goods: cloth, spices, oil for lamps, dyes, and wine. He did not own ships, but he brokered their lading, he bought and sold and made a great fortune. I do not remember that time, or only a mere wisp. I have the notion that we lived in a beautiful house far from the great rivers. I have no recollection of ever seeing the ships and wharves and great warehouses that made my father's wealth. Of that time I only recall one event: a birthday, which was of course also the anniversary of my mother's passing. Great sadness in the house, as tho my coming into the world had been a tragedy."

Michal was quiet a long while, staring out the window, as if she might catch some sight of her childhood in the churning clouds above.

"My father is a clever, shrewd man. His fortune waxed, and he invested in lands here in the west of the state. Great fields of wheat and corn surrounded our home. We might as well have been on an island in the south seas, for all the contact I had with the rest of humanity. Then he sold those lands, making a pretty profit I'm sure, and he bought this tract. I have lived here for six years, his prisoner."

She got up and returned to the wooden platform

where she poses and said, "But I will not live here the rest of my days. I swear that. My hope is to see again the city where I was born. I will not live in this wilderness. I will not spend all my days alone with him."

She sighed deeply, as tho steeling herself for a terrible blow, and resumed the pose of mourning. She spoke on, much quieter now. "When he tells me how much I resemble my mother, I feel a blackness descend. I cannot bear it any longer."

She became silent. And I returned to my work.

October 18

The messenger boy came for me early and said I must follow. We wandered through the house, but left it and walked up the path toward the hill. I had spent so much time indoors of late, the landscape seemed peculiar. The leaves are all of color, gold and orange and scarlet. The smell of autumn is ripe in the air. I had forgotten, it seemed, that there was a world outside the studio and the snaking corridors of the mansion house.

We ascended the hill, and I knew he was taking me to the cave. I asked why I must go. He remained mum. I told him I would go no further without a proper answer. "You must come."

I stopped and said in certain terms that I would not return to that hateful place.

"The young mistress is there. She requires your presence."

I asked why, but he would only say, "You must come."

And so I went. The way seemed shorter this day, as is always the case when journeying to a loathed place. Too soon we passed by Jack Smoke's shanty. Too soon we saw the black gaping maw of the cave. "The master is inside. And the mistress," my guide said. Fearing the cave too, he would not enter. He pointed into the shadows, as tho it were the entryway to hell and hid a thousand devils.

I heard a faint sound from within, Michal's pleading voice I thought, and entered.

I had no candle nor lantern today, but a short distance into the cave I saw a pool of reddish light. I went that way, picking my path with care. As daylight faded behind me, the voices grew louder. It was Michal and John Good, disputing.

Hearing the anguish in her voice, I hurried. "Never, never, never, never!" she was crying.

I ran now, heedless of the rough and twisting pathway. More times than I could count, I banged my head and stumbled to the cave's floor. But soon I emerged into the great chamber, and there were father and daughter. Three lanterns burned in the vast open space, one hanging from the wall and the others on a great raised platform of stone.

Father and daughter turned to face me. The strange illumination made them both ghastly, red-faced, and quaking in the lantern's light. Tho they'd ceased speaking, it seemed that the echoes of their quarrel still flitted like bats around the great chamber. A crazed light shone in Michal's eyes.

As I came near, John Good's posture and expression changed, as if he were taking on a new role. "You've come," he said. "You can inspect Esra and Chester's work then." I told him I didn't understand. "There," he said, pointing to the large platform-like place. "I've had them up here the last week clearing away stone, cutting and hauling. Their work is not quite done, but you've instructed them well. I was afraid all their pounding might bring the entire cave down on their heads. But as you can see, they've done good work."

Approaching, I did see that this place was different from the rest of the cave. The gnarled icicles of stone had been hacked off the ceiling and the floor was chipped and chiseled flat. They'd driven a few iron staples into the walls from which to hang lanterns.

"This will be the place where the monument shall stand," John Good said. "Here my dear one shall rest until the Day of Judgment. Here, I hope also to have my final rest, with your memorial figure standing guard." He took my hand, eager as a treasure-hunter showing off his trove. "There we three will rest." He pointed to a rough indentation in the cave wall. "You and your boys will carve me out a fine tomb there. Deep into the rock wall. Secure as a fortress. I have already a bronze caster in Manhattan at work on the door. Soon enough it will head north on the Hudson and then go west on an Erie barge and then by wagon here. When you've shaped the tomb and the smith has built in the hinges, I'll have the door hauled up here and put in place."

I had never seen John Good so filled with delight. His great house, his vast land holdings, his army of laborers and servants were nothing in comparison to his tomb.

"You'll have to superintend Esra and Chester when they begin widening the cave mouth. It must be a beautiful entranceway."

"Father," Michal said quietly. "I want to go back to the house." No wheedling and winding him around her finger today. She was begging. Here in the cave, all of her power over John Good was as naught. "Let me go," she whispered. "I want to go back."

"First show me how the memorial will look. Get up there," John Good commanded. Michal refused. "Stand there where the monument will stand for all time. Go — take your place so that I can see."

"Father, please," Michal begged. "I want to leave."

"Go!" he shouted. "Stand there as you'll stand in stone forever." He took hold of her by the arm and ushered her to the raised platform. Weeping now, Michal climbed the two rough steps and took her place. She didn't need to be told to strike the tribulation pose. Grief was no role this day. Affliction, and terror even, were as natural to her now as breathing.

John Good is a tyrant and his persecution of Michal

is awful to witness, but he does have an eye for true beauty. Standing there slumped with mourning, with the light of the lantern bathing her white skin and white gown in swaths of shimmering light, she might have been a dire angel. The only sound I heard then was the far-off drip of water.

We — all three of us — were helpless then. John Good was enchained by the sight of Michal. She was trapped in his vision of what must be. And I was, as I remain, a prisoner to them both.

"She is beautiful," John Good finally said. "She is perfect." With that the spell was broken and we fled the cave for daylight.

October 19

Back to work on the statue today, after spending a few hours with Chester and Esra and going down to the stable to see Nessie.

Michal says nothing. Alone in the studio, I hoped she might speak more. But what happened yesterday has hurt her in a manner I do not understand. Two days ago she asked about Little Sion and the people I know there and was eager to hear about Mr. Bonness and Watty. "Anything but this place. Anywhere but here," she'd said. But today she is silent as the cave.

October 19 (later)

As I write, it is well past midnight. My candle burns low. Still, I hunch over it to keep anyone outside from seeing its light. I know it ridiculous, but the mansion house is so silent now I fear the scratching of my quill on this page might wake John Good's men.

I have seen Michal. I have been to her chambers. We have sat together and conspired a plan.

At dinner this evening one of the serving girls tucked a small scrap of paper under my soup bowl. By her expression and the way she sidled away after delivering the message, I knew I must keep it secret.

Returning to my room, I opened the note and read: "We must speak tonight. Come to my apartments. My father is gone for the time to deal with a tenant's property dispute. Mrs. Strand sleeps like the dead." It was signed "Michal" and to it was attached a map of the mansion house. An X marked her chamber, and a fine line in red pencil showed me the way.

So when it seemed the house was finally quiet, I set off.

The path wound this way and that, like the chambers of the great cave. I went, silent as dust, down the corridors. There is a wind tonight, and it sighs in the chimneys and around the unfinished window frames. Indeed there is a constant movement of air, as tho the house itself were breathing.

Cupping my candle so that it barely lit my next step, I went careful and slow upwards. Michal's chambers are on the top floor of the north wing, past John Good's great study and library, past the sitting room which Michal has told me is never used, for no guests ever come to Goodspell.

Up I rose, along a stairway that moaned beneath my feet. With each step, I imagined one of John Good's men lunging out at me, shouting threats. But I was alone on that stairway, and alone down the long hallway, and alone until I came to Michal's door. It was ajar and a faint band of light flickered on the floor. I whispered her name, and she hurried to admit me.

When the door was closed behind us, she lit more candles for her lantern. The room is not like the others in the mansion house. Whereas my chamber has rough board walls and floor, hers is like the queen's chamber in a castle. Tapestries hang on the walls, a beautiful carpet (she has told me it came all the way from Persia!) covers the floor, and her bedposts are carved in most wonderful patterns. There are two chairs and a desk. And her window looks out on a broad view.

The moon is still up as I write these words. But seen from Michal's window, it was a most gorgeous orb. Casting watery light over the far-off hills, it seemed more a kind of radiant fruit than the dead stone of the night sky.

"You've come, you've come," she repeated, as tho I were some rescuing knight.

We sat and I asked her why she'd summoned me.

"I cannot abide this place," she said simply. She showed me the book she'd been reading while she awaited me. It was mostly engravings: views of cathedrals in France, the high mountains of the Alps, Scottish moorlands, the gardens of Copenhagen, the great rock of Gibraltar. "I will not live another week here, Albion. It is unbearable, to live this dungeon life."

I inspected the book for a moment, then looked around at her chamber. No girls in Little Sion, nor Mrs. Bonness, had ever seen such furnishings. To live amidst such beauty would be as a glorious dream. I told Michal this. She responded with a groan and a shake of her head.

"But they are free! They may have work and the work, I know, can be a heavy burden. But there are times of freedom. An hour there, an hour here, they can go to visit their friends. They can walk the lane with no one dogging their steps. They have moments of freedom when no one demands anything of them."

I allowed that this was true, but still, I told her, every girl I knew would surely give up the chance to gossip with friends to live in such a beautiful place.

"It is beautiful," she said. "I have all the lovely baubles my father's money can buy. But still I must leave."

She pointed to the lantern on her desk. It was a

pretty thing, of silver and glass. She placed her hands over the lantern, closing off the air. Her eyes screwed down and her lips trembled, touching the hot metal. But still she held on while the candle flame flickered, struggled, and then died.

Then she took my hand and pressed it to her breast. "I must leave him or I will die. I'll die as surely as that candle flame dies when it has no air."

We heard a noise in the hallway and fell silent. But no footsteps came.

She clutched my hand tighter. "I must leave this place forever," she whispered. "And you must come with me. You must be my guide. Take me back to your Little Sion."

I was of course dumbfounded. The two of us could not just walk away from Goodspell. And even if we were allowed to leave, the journey back was fraught with uncertainty and peril.

Trying to dissuade her, however, was useless. "I have thought on this for years, Albion. I have dreamed and planned and made preparations. But I knew I could not effect my plan alone." Still she held my hand tight, as tho afraid that I might flee and never return. "I have prayed for release, Albion, prayed that I might be free. More than one time I have come close to taking my own life. He is insufferable. I have sworn to myself, sworn to God, that I will not live out my life this way. Better the grave than this living tomb."

"Perhaps you can persuade him, that at the end of my service here, you might accompany me back home. I'm sure Mrs. Bonness would be pleased to have you as a guest."

She shook her head, grim as the angel of death. "You will not be allowed to return, Albion. You, too, are his prisoner."

I argued that this was impossible. "Your father does not have that right," I said.

"But he has the power. When you finish the statue, you will be forced to begin another. And another will follow. Unless you flee with me, you will be here all the days of your life."

Finally, she let go of my hand. "I have made plans, Albion. I have made preparations. And I have other allies here. My father gives me beautiful objects, so many that he has lost track. Some of these I have already given as gifts. And others remain: silver chains, lockets, precious stones. With these, we can buy our freedom."

It is madness, I told her. It is impossible for us to flee back to Little Sion without being caught. And even if we succeeded, John Good would go straight there, searching for us. Could Mr. Bonness or the Reverend Mr. Yates protect us from such a man consumed with wrath? Even speaking of a plan was dangerous folly. If we are prisoners now, how much heavier will the chains be if John Good knows we desire escape?

"Listen to me closely, Albion. This is no jest, no exaggeration. If you do not help me to flee, then all my hope will be gone. And without hope there is no reason to live any longer. If I truly believed I must live my life this way forever, then I would throw myself down a well."

She does not lie. I know that. As I write these words now, in my cell, I know in my heart she will take her own life if I do not help her to flee. But to flee might just as well bring us both to death's door. God help me.

October 21

No entry yesterday. I could not bring quill to page. Indeed I hid my journal in amongst the tools and trash of the stoneshop. For the first time I fear John Good reading these words. If he comes upon the entry for two days past, he will surely lock Michal away as tho she were a true prisoner and Goodspell the most awful fortress keep.

She came to the studio and I worked, but the statue took on new meaning now. It was like Michal herself, frozen, unable to move. I hammered and brushed away the dust and chips. I aimed the chisel point and swung. But instead of freeing the form that lurked within, somehow I was making her more a prisoner.

We spoke nothing of her plan, as tho our midnight meeting had not occurred. Mrs. Strand is not in the room, but she sits with her ear to the door, I'm sure.

October 22

Michal's expression grows desperate. At one point this morning, John Good burst in upon us and I was certain that he had discovered all. Michal stared at him, as if expecting accusations, threats, instant punishment. But he merely came, he said, to see the progress of the statue. Declaring it to his liking, he just as suddenly was gone.

As soon as the door closed, she left her place on the platform and came to me. Whispering, she said, "Soon, soon. I have spoken with my friends here, and given away my most valuable brooch. Soon we will be away."

October 22 (later)

I have before me now the letter she gave me today. In it, she outlines her plan. It is a foolhardy scheme, certain to fail. However, I know that she speaks the truth about taking her own life if she must remain here at Goodspell.

Two parts of the plan seem most liable to failure. With a few dozen men in his employ, John Good can certainly make a formidable search party. Many of these men have spent their lives in this area and know all the trails and paths and byways. How can we — a mere girl and I, a stranger to this place — hope to elude them? And even if this miracle should happen, how could we survive the trek back to Little Sion? I know it is north, a week's journey. But without food, a compass, or guidance, it seems we must perish along the way. Michal is determined, however. She will have her freedom or meet her end in the attempt.

I will hide the journal again, in a different place. Neither Esra nor Chester can read, but they might stumble upon it and show it to John Good.

October 23

Another day of labor, but my heart most certainly is not in the work. Again, John Good burst in upon us. Today it was during a period of rest. Michal sat and stared out the window, as tho she might see all the way to Little Sion. I was brushing crumbs of stone off the arm I was shaping. The door slammed back, and there stood John Good. Did he think he might discover us in some secret plotting? Did he know that I had visited Michal by night? It seems some powerful jealousy gnaws at his heart, thinking me a rival for her affections.

Whatever the case, what he caught us in was entirely innocent. He inspected the statue briefly, nodded his approval, and exhorted me not to dawdle. "The end draws near," he said. "You've conjured a perfect likeness out of the stone. But you must finish soon."

October 24

Michal did not come to the studio today. The messenger boy delivered me a note from John Good. "Proceed with your efforts. My daughter will not be joining you. I'm sure you can continue without a live model."

I did work, and John Good is correct that I might finish the monument without seeing her again. The entire form is there, the shape of her clothing and hair too. But the face remains only in rough form.

After working for a few hours, it became clear that without her presence my eye grows dim and my hand grows weak. I can shape the face, an approximation, but it will not be Michal.

Distracted by these thoughts, my swing went awry, and I nearly caused grievous damage to her right hand. I paused, trembling. One careless hammer blow, and weeks of work can be destroyed.

For a moment I toyed with this idea, picturing the hammer pounding the statue to a pile of rubble. I would not even need to bar the door. In moments I could destroy the statue. Why these thoughts tho? Do I hate my work? No, but I hate what purpose it will be put to.

The chisel fell from my hand with a bell-like clatter. Without another thought, I left that place and hurried to John Good's great study room. Servants stared as I passed them in the corridor. William Williams, whom I had not seen in weeks, asked why I was in that part of the house. But I pushed past him and, without knocking, entered John Good's chamber.

He was, as I had pictured him, at the great table with books and engravings and papers strewn around like drifts of snow. "Where is Michal?" I demanded.

For a moment, he was confused by my sudden explosion of feeling. But regaining his composure, he said in an icy commanding voice, "Go back to work, Mr. Straight. My daughter's whereabouts are not your concern."

"If I am to finish the monument, then Michal must be there."

"Having inspected the statue a number of times, I am satisfied that her presence is no longer necessary."

"I will be the one to decide that," I said, surprising him, and myself, by the force of my reply. "The face is only in the rough form. Without Michal there, the expression will be false."

"Go back to your work," he said, as if dismissing a rude or impertinent servant. "There are matters I must attend to."

"You must attend now to me," I said. Only then did I realize that I still held my hammer. It was heavy in my grip. For a moment I saw myself charging at John Good like an Iroquois warrior, the hammer raised as a war club. Such madness, such rage, I felt.

John Good is a large man, and I have not yet reached my full height. But having swung the hammer for three years, and hoisted blocks of stone and cut cords of firewood, I possess a fair amount of strength. And the heat of anger can give a boy the courage of a man.

I did not throw myself on him, however. That would serve no good purpose. I strode to his table and pushed the papers and books onto the floor.

Just then men appeared in the door behind me. They rushed toward me, but John Good told them to halt. "Leave us," he said. They hesitated. "Go. Mr. Straight and I have important matters to discuss." The men seemed relieved, unsure how they were to assist him.

When the door closed, John Good said to me, "Put down the hammer." I hesitated, but obeyed. "Now attend to my words, Albion Straight. Michal will no longer be standing for you as a model. I have discovered certain facts which make this no longer wise. Namely, it has come to my attention that items of her jewelry have been found in the possession of house maids and at least one of the carpenter's boys. When these servants were brought to task, they all said the items were given, not stolen. I believe this. Michal has a spiteful nature at times. When she is hot with anger she will do foolish acts to injure me. The jewelry found among the servants was my wife's. I gave it to Michal as a sacred trust. I wanted her to wear my wife's finest ornaments so that I might remember. And where do I find it? Around the neck of a common scullery maid."

By the look on his face I knew he did not regard me in the same way as these other servants. "I tell you all this so that you might understand and be able to complete the work you've begun for me." He stooped and found a paper amongst those on the floor. "This is the contract you signed on September 18. I will honor that contract. It is plain to me that your presence here has been a disruption. The work you've done is most excellent and will serve as a fitting memorial. But as soon as you have finished it, you will leave this place."

There it was, the words I'd longed to hear, and yet they came as a death sentence to a condemned man. I could finish the statue in a day or two if I worked steadily.

I could be on the way home before the snow flew. Yet to hear him say this vexed my heart extremely.

"It was with great sorrow that I laid these accusations before Michal. She denied nothing, waiting for the punishment which she knew must follow. You've come to know her, Albion. You've studied her beauty well enough to capture it in stone. So you, more than anyone else, can understand how much it grieves me to chasten her for her misdeeds. I told her that she can no longer see you. And this, I think, is a far worse punishment than anything I've inflicted on her thus far. I have suspicions that she was bribing the servants in hopes of making some foolhardy flight from this, her home. I also suspect that knowing you and speaking with you and learning of your life has incited her to these evil thoughts of fleeing me."

He did not accuse me, nor wait for a confession. It mattered nothing to him what might my role be in Michal's dream of escape.

"More than anything in the world, it grieves me to punish my daughter. Afterward she will not speak to me, or even look me in the eye. After I've given her what she deserves, she will not respond in any way to me, as tho I do not even exist. Perhaps you are the only one who can begin to understand how painful this is for me. But I must punish her! I must! I cannot allow anything which might separate her from me."

Again he held up the contract I'd signed back in Little Sion. "I will pay you the amount stated here, a hundred dollars, upon completion of the statue. And then I will have one of my men guide you to the main route north. You can be home in a week."

With that, our interview ended, and as I write these words I am torn as I never have been before. I can leave, richer than any boy has a right to be. I can be home in a week. But if I leave, then Michal will be trapped here. And I am certain she told me the truth when she said she could not bear to live this way any longer.

October 25

I worked as in a daze today, smoothing the stone of her arms with a file, then giving the final polish to the flowing shapes of her garment. The face is unfinished however. The outline is there. Indeed it does capture

Michal's expression. But there are small details yet undone. The studio's silence weighs like a millstone around my neck.

October 25 (later)

It was sheer folly I know, but I could no longer stand the empty silence. I could no longer endure the thought of Michal alone in her room, considering how best to end her life.

So I waited this night until the house was silent. Then I waited a while longer, and set off down the dark halls to her chambers.

Around every corner I thought I saw one of John Good's men. On the stairway, a cat scooted by and set my heart hammering in my chest.

I paused a long while before rapping on Michal's door. Perhaps, I thought, John Good had moved her to some new room where I would never find her. Perhaps he waited there to trap me. Perhaps he now lurked in that room, in that bed.

But I'd come this far and would not turn back. I tapped quietly on the door and received no answer. I tapped again and heard a stirring within. I put my hand on the latch and opened the door a crack. A rustle of bedsheets came to my ear, and then a groan. I entered the room.

"Go away," Michal said, in a voice of abject despair.

A few red embers glowed in her little fireplace. As my eyes adjusted to the warm light, I saw that she was hunched up in bed, her arms fastened tight around her knees.

"Michal," I said, quiet as a the fall of a leaf.

"Albion? Is that you?" A note of hope, of life, returned to her voice. "Albion, have you come?"

I went to where she sat and took her hand. It was cold, as tho she'd already taken her life. The chill of her skin, the emptiness of her voice, the way she crouched, folded in on herself: all of these combined to strengthen the thought. Was she no longer among the living?

But I chased this awful notion from my mind, pressing her hand and assuring her that it was I who'd come.

"Your father —" I began. But oh, how I hated those

words. Better tyrant, or persecutor, better monster or jailer, than father. "John Good," I began again, "has told me I might leave as soon as the statue is complete. He will pay me my full wage and send me home."

"Then go," she said, despair again welling up in her voice. "Take your money. You've earned it. And go."

She tried to pull her hand away, but I held on firm and steady. "No. I cannot leave you here alone."

We were silent a long while. The embers in the hearth throbbed weakly. Their light barely reached us. Michal's face was blurred and indistinct, as tho she'd become the statue, yet unfinished.

"You must leave. That is my father's will. He has forbidden me to see you again. As long as you remain here, I will be locked away in this part of the house. I am forbidden to go outside, to eat in the dining room, even to visit the room where he studies. If you leave, at least I will have some tiny scrap of freedom again."

"I will buy your freedom," I said. "I will trade my labor for your release. If I promise him another statue, or memorials carved in the cave walls, or some grander work, he might accept it as payment for your release."

At first this seemed to spark her anger. "I am not a mere object to be bought and sold!" Too loud, much too loud, was her voice. This little outburst stabbed a little spear of dread into her heart. "You must leave now, Albion," she continued in a whisper. "Go. Mrs. Strand sleeps like the dead, but since I have been found out, my father has men keeping an eye and an ear on me. Go now. Finish the statue and take your money and leave this place."

"No. He told me he wants the cave to be a tribute, every inch of the walls carved as a memorial. If I promise him that I'll complete that work, he might relent and let you free."

Suddenly, she put her finger to my lips. "They are coming," she whispered. "Go, please go."

She was right, of course. Footsteps pounded down the hallway. Voices rose. I heard Mrs. Strand's angry whine, and the hubbub of servants and John Good loudest of all.

The door slammed back and in they came, with lanterns painting their faces a demon red.

"Get away from her!" John Good bellowed like an ox. He lunged at me and, with one of his men assisting, pulled me away from Michal. Soon they had me in the corridor with shouts and cursing. I turned once as I was dragged away and caught a last glimpse of Michal. Again the veil of despair had fallen over her face. Hopeless and helpless, she watched as I was taken away from her.

I write these words now in my cell. One of John Good's men stands guard outside the door. I will be watched tomorrow as I finish the statue and then marched like a prisoner to the track which leads north to Little Sion. And I will never seen Michal again.

The last entry

Those last words were written two months ago. I pick up the quill again to finish the story. The events of those days are blurred in my memory, but I will tell what happened the best I can.

I slept not at all that night after I was caught in Michal's chamber. After writing my last entry, I puffed a few breaths on the ink to make certain it was dry. Then I closed the journal and hoped never to look inside these pages again. It was, I thought, a record of doom, of failure, and of despair. I could not conceive of wanting ever to read the words again.

Lighting all the candles I had left, I had a bright little blaze before me. I thought to burn the journal, as a way of destroying my memories of this awful time, page upon page leading to this grievous end.

I held the journal over the flames, which combined like strands of a fiery rope. Even as I write these words I see the evidence of that heat. One corner of this journal is singed black.

But I hesitated. I pulled the book away. I sniffed at the air and caught a different kind of burnt scent. Opening my door, I saw a long tendril of smoke descending from the stairway. My guard was gone. And from far away, I heard shouts of alarm.

Without a glance behind me, I ran. Down the hall I went, up a stairway, across the dining room, and around a great curving corridor. It wasn't until I reached Michal's room that I knew where I was headed. By this time the smoke was heavy in the air, churning and twisting like angry ghosts.

The shouts and the clatter of buckets came from

nearby. I hurried to the window and looked down to see a dozen men struggling to put out the blaze. Flames were eating at the wall of this wing, rising even as I stood there.

But where was Michal? Had John Good come to fetch her as soon as he was aware of the fire? Had she bolted, as I had when the men were drawn away to fight the blaze?

Books and clothing were strewn on the floor. Michal's bed was a tangle, one of its curtains ripped away. Only as I reached to pull back the bed sheets did I realize that I still held my journal. Clothes and tools I'd left behind. But this book, which only a few moments before I was about to burn, was all that I carried.

Now the noise of the blaze was loud, like the growling of a fierce beast. I ran from the room and down the stairs. I headed away from the fire, through the labyrinth of halls and chambers and finally found myself in my studio.

Lit by the red quake of flame-light the statue of Michal stood. I paused a moment, regarding my work for the last time. Her white skin, her white gown, were painted crimson.

"I hoped you'd come here." My shock, at hearing her voice, set my thoughts into wild disarray. Was I mad, hearing cold stone speak? Was this all a nightmare? But again I heard Michal's voice. "Come away from the window."

No, I wasn't bereft of my senses. Michal hid in the shadow of the statue. She took my hand and drew me, too, into the darkness.

"Rest here a moment," she whispered. I asked how she'd gotten there, how she'd escaped John Good. But she shushed me with a finger to my lips. "No one will see us. We'll go out a way I know."

Still, questions boiled in me as the gathering smoke boiled in the air. Again, I asked, and again she bade me hold my tongue. She pressed her mouth close to mine ear. "We'll wait just a bit longer, until all his men are out with their buckets."

The noise of the fire ebbed and rose, as ocean waves might. Tired to the bone, confused and afraid, I waited for Michal's signal. Finally, as a tin dinner horn sounded the fire alarm, we got up from our hiding place and fled from that room.

I turned back, however, and took up my hammer. Why I brought it away is still unclear, unless it was a desire that John Good never touch it. Or did I think that by taking the hammer, the statue of Michal would remain forever unfinished? Whatever the reason, I carried it with me as we fled from the mansion house.

She told me later that she'd spent many hours exploring the great building. At times when her governess would nap, Michal would wander the byways and secret halls of the mansion house. She knew the stairs which led from kitchen to dining room, the narrow corridors which connected one unfinished room to another. And so we were able to pass through the house quickly and unseen.

Out a back door we emerged, on the side of the house far from the fire. Soon we were climbing the hill which led to the cave. My feelings (fear rising to panic) gnawed at me as we ascended the trail. And my thoughts, too, were a terrible jumble. We might escape for an hour or two. But to hide out in the cave would be madness. We had no food, no warm clothing, nothing to make a fire with. For a moment I was stricken with the thought that she still was intent on taking her life. And that she hoped that I might join her in this awful task.

We paused once on our ascent, and looked down through the trees — now shed of their leaves — at the great fiery catastrophe. One of John Good's engravings shows a religious pilgrim guided by a beautiful lady. They pause, looking down from a heavenly peak on the eternal flame and smoke of hell. Now Goodspell might have been that infernal place. Michal took my hand, to steady me I suppose, and we gazed down at her home and prison. I knew that buried in that crimson chaos was my statue of Michal. She stood in the flames, in her eternal pose of grief and mourning, unmindful of the fire around her.

The tin trumpet blew another long and desperate note, and I wondered if this could have been the sound that had so many times woken Watty from his uneasy sleep.

Michal tugged on my hand and we kept climbing.

Our destination was not, I soon discovered, the cave mouth, but the shanty of Jack Smoke. The little hut was dark. Still, Michal led me there with no hesitation. I tried to dissuade her, thinking of the stories I'd heard of the man's viciousness and bloody rages. "Lies," she said. "All lies."

We ducked under the door frame and waited a moment. In some ways the shanty was more grim than the cave. The reek of animal skins and whiskey was heavy. The ceiling hung so low I could not stand up straight.

The floor was bare dirt, a-tumble with bones and leaves and cooking trash. I might have thought it a wild beast's den, if I hadn't seen a man living here weeks before.

"He'll be here soon," Michal said.

"I be here right now," came a reply from the shadows. Jack Smoke rose and approached.

I came between him and Michal, but she reassured me. "He's my friend," she said. "Before you came here, he was my only friend. He's going to help us get away."

And so Michal's plan was discovered to me. She had, when chance allowed it, come up the hill to visit this strange little man. In the six years since she'd arrived here, the visits were infrequent. She had needed to be so very careful in these secret forays. Indeed, she was drawn to Jack Smoke precisely because there was so much bad blood between him and her father. She came when she could, and they spent pleasurable hours talking together. But her goal was always to escape Goodspell. And to that end, Jack Smoke was a willing partner.

I asked Michal later why such a man would want to spend time with the likes of her. "Perhaps he was lonely. He always seemed so happy to see me. Or perhaps he merely wanted to besmirch the one thing my father held dear. I truly believe my father would have throttled the life out of me, if he knew I snuck up here to visit Jack. My father had taken most everything away from him. All this land was his once. He wanted to hurt my father in the worst way possible."

So they planned her escape. And when I arrived, it seemed the fortunate sign. I could lead her away safely if Jack Smoke remained behind to muddy our trail.

Most of the servants were terrified to carry a message to him. But there was one girl still who remained loyal to Michal. And for the mere gift of a small velvet ribbon, she ran out to Jack's shanty and told him that this was the night.

Long he'd planned how he might repay John Good for his terrible acts. Long he'd pondered his revenge. And so at Michal's signal, all was in place. Daubs of pitch, dry pine shavings, handfuls of birch bark were set in their places, and the flame of a small candle was then all he needed to bring down the great house.

And now, in Jack Smoke's shanty, he prepared us for our escape. Michal had stolen various cups and forks, books and papers, even a pair of her father's best boots. And on his occasional trips to a trading post at Wellsville,

Jack would barter them for more useful items. Now he equipped us with a carrying pack, blankets, flint and steel, heavy Indian shoes to replace her flimsy slippers. Seeing that I had none, he gave me his coat. "I can trade for another one with the swag Michal's got me," he said.

"You best get on the trail while it's still dark," he told us. "I'll head down to the house and pretend I'm spying on the fire. Sure thing one of the men will snatch me and drag me up to the great man. And I'll act all feared and scary and spill out a whole story about seeing you go down the west trail. Meanwhile, you go east a bit, like I showed you, and then up past the deer lick and the Red Bank trail. He'll come after you. No doubt about it. Once the fire is out, or even maybe before, he'll come a-looking for you. But I figure you got yourself a day or two headstart on them. Far as I know, nobody but you's aware of the way I shown you. You get a little good luck, and I tell a good story, and you might get clean away."

With a warm press of my hand and a tender embrace for Michal, he set off toward the mansion house. "You get on going," he said. "You know the way."

Indeed she did, at least the first little bit. Even in the dark, she followed the trail as sure as a Indian scout. On her visits, he'd taken her here. He'd told her to hold it close in her mind, for one day she'd need to follow the path without his guidance.

And so we set off. We walked the way he told us, Michal leading by picking landmarks out of the darkness. A great oak loomed ahead, its leaves rattling and hissing like a snake. Beyond that we followed a creek bed of layered shale. Then we passed a hollow log where, Michal said, she and Jack Smoke came in the proper season to steal honey from the hive.

Soon, however, we were beyond the places she knew. By this time dawn was seeping a feverish pink into the sky. Neither Michal nor I had slept at all that night and now were stumbling and listing like drunken ghosts. At one point she tripped and landed in the leaves. I bent to help her up but she said she couldn't move, couldn't take another step without sleep. And so we hid ourselves a short distance from the trail, in a little bower under the branches of a crimson sumac, and we slept.

I was first to wake, rising from a dream of fire. The pictures tattered and blew away as I roused myself. However one image, as distinct as an engraving, lingered in my mind. It was Michal, in the pose she'd struck for our statue. But she was flesh and blood, not cold stone. Fire swirled and swept around her, and she was motionless, helpless to escape.

The sun was near the noon-point. The air, however, had lost none of its chill. Indeed, it seemed that a vast breath of cold air was bearing down on us from the north.

I woke Michal, and we broke a johnnycake and ate in silence. Then we gathered our belongings and set out. I considered leaving the hammer behind, burying it perhaps in a shallow grave. For what use would a stonecutter's hammer be in the forest? It can cut no firewood, kill no game for food, strike no fire. But it was all I had left of my time with Mr. Bonness. If I should never see him again, I might remember him by it.

Up to this point, she had been the guide, but now we were in terrain which neither of us knew. We had a trail for a long while, and Jack Smoke's instructions. We could keep to a northern course by the position of the sun. Nonetheless, our notion of place and direction faded quickly.

For much of that day, we trekked in silence. Always, I had my ears pricked to catch the sound of pursuit. Unlike the slave-masters he so much resembled, John Good did not have hunting hounds. There would be no baying and yapping to tell us how far behind our pursuers were.

"Jack can tell a convincing lie," Michal said. "At least for a while they'll follow the trail which goes the other way. He'll whine and beg and cower, and my father will believe it at first. But he'll go out on horse, and after he's traveled well past the place we might have reached, he'll know that he's been deceived. I hate to think the price that Jack will pay for his treachery."

And then he'd head our way. Or perhaps he had already sent some scouts and trackers to the east. I told Michal it wasn't very far to Little Sion. "A few days' walk and we'll be there," I said, trying to make my voice sound sure. But truly, wandering with no beaten path to follow, I didn't know how long the journey would take.

That night the snow came. Michal huddled against me, and we wrapped the blanket around us like a butterfly's cocoon. The wind rose and thrashed at the trees. First a few flakes, and then swirls of white snow flashed out of the nightblack sky. We considered making a fire, for Jack Smoke had given me flint and steel and even a tinder box. However, it seemed we were still too close to Goodspell to take that risk.

We rested on a bed of leaves and pine needles. Michal had a rag around her head to keep her ears warm, and I sat with my hands clamped between my legs. "My father will not give up his hunt. Never, never give up. He told me more than once that if I were gone, he would take his own life. He told me that his love for me was all that kept him alive. He will search until the last day of his life."

This was the first sign of her weakening will. Back at Goodspell she had seemed utterly set on escape. But now, cold and hungry and lost, her desperate longing for freedom was fading.

She didn't say then that our flight was hopeless. But I heard a note of despair in her voice. "He told me once that I should never find a husband and marry. And if I did, he'd hunt the man down, 'hunt him to the ends of the earth' is how he put it, and kill him like a wolf that had stolen and gorged on his sheep. So I have done a very bad thing, Albion. I've hurt my father in a way that can never be repaired, and I've brought certain doom on your head."

I told her this was folly. Soon we'd be in Little Sion. Soon we'd be under the protection of Mr. Bonness and the Reverend Mr. Yates. She was no longer a little girl. In the eyes of God she was free to choose how she might live.

"He's still my father," she said, through chattering teeth.

I told her we needed to rest and got up to make a kind of burrow in the leaves. Soon we were out of the wind and half-buried. So we pressed together and did the best we could to steal some sleep. She wept some. The tears made the cold worse. And she coughed, a weak rattling sound like a bird fluttering inside a cage.

The next day we trudged northward. By doling out our little stock of food, I reckoned we had enough for a week. But already it seemed we'd gone too far to the east and had lost a day. Steering by the sun and by pure instinct, we did however find a better trail that afternoon. There were wagon ruts in the frozen mud, and we followed these to a farm. Seeing the squat little shanty, a pang of hope pierced my heart. Surely these good people might give us shelter and food.

The door of the hut was open. We looked inside and again our hopes fell like the plummet of the heavy wet snowflakes. It was abandoned: no tenants and no food.

But the last occupants had left a few sticks of firewood and the chimney looked serviceable. We both were wet, and I worried that Michal might collapse and refuse to go any farther. So I took the chance and made a small fire.

In the gray cloudy sky, dropping puffs and waves of snow, a small plume of chimney smoke might not be seen. And perhaps, I reasoned, we were far enough away that it was safe.

Thus I made a fire and as we warmed ourselves the weight of Michal's despair seemed to lift.

Jack Smoke had wrapped a piece of salt pork in cabbage leaves. I poked a stick through the meat, and in a short while we had a small repast of pork and corn cake, with snow for water.

"Tell me what you'll do when you reach Manhattan," I asked her. For this was her plan now: a brief stop in Little Sion, then north to the canal and seaward to the great city.

At first she did not reply. But the food and warmth were like the rain and sun of springtime. And she opened like a flower.

"I suppose most girls would want to see the shops

with all their wonderful clothing. I've had that, even at Goodspell. I had fine clothes and beautiful baubles. I think I should go to the wharves and see the great ships. And I'd inquire whither they were headed. This one to London and this one to China and this one to Jamaica and this one to India. And I'd choose the ship that was going farthest from this place and I'd buy my passage and never return." Her smile faded some. "I'd go to a place where my father should never find me."

What had begun as a happy fancy slipped into darkness. Again, her thoughts led her to escape. Always, with Michal, there was the notion of going away, going far and never coming back.

We finished our small dinner and then gathered up leaves for a bed. The door of the shanty gaped open and the chinking between the logs of the walls had fallen out in places. Still, this place was like a palace compared to where we'd slept the night before.

In the night, she grew feverish. Her moans woke me and I felt of her forehead. It burned, and I had not medicine, nor knowledge of doctoring — nothing to help her.

The next morning we were off before the sun came up. Our supply of food was dwindling quickly. I knew we must find a farm soon or perish. Perhaps, I thought, we might beg a meal. Or even scour over a cornfield and find a few ears left behind. The kernels would be hard as flint, but they might soften in our bellies and calm the growling.

Where were we, I asked myself, and how should we get back to the main trail? True, I could see the place of the sun in the sky and aim us north. But we traveled terrain that seemed to have known no civilizing influence. This trail we walked was likely one which Seneca warriors had taken on their bloody raids into Pennsylvania. As yet the great trees stood, ready for the ax. The streams were undammed, yet to be harnessed for the mill. Here and there we passed a small field where I suppose the Senecas had grown their corn and beans. Since our war of independence, however, the natives had been driven west and into Canada.

The hammer grew heavier with every passing mile, but never once did Michal say I should lay it by. Useless, like a broken millstone, it surely slowed our progress.

Still, I could not give it up. At one point, perhaps touched by Michal's fever, I thought of it as a kind of lodestone that might point north and show us the proper direction home. But this foolish notion passed.

At a spot by the side of a rocky ravine, we found an apple tree with some shrunken fruit still hanging. We collected some of these and gnawed at them as we walked.

Again with food in her belly, Michal's voice returned. "He's not far behind us," she said, bleak and weary. "He's on our trail as surely as the sun goes up and down. His hunters will have combed the grounds around the mansion house by this time and will have found our path. They will travel faster than we can. A boy and a girl cannot outrun men who've lived their whole lives hunting and trapping this place."

I tried to argue these thoughts away. But she would hear none of it. "My father will not sleep until he has me again." Still we trudged on. Still she did not give up.

The snow had ceased by then, but the air stayed hard and cold as iron. Twice the trail withered away into nothing, and we blundered about the brush, lost. Both times that day, however, we did manage to find the trail again, or perhaps it was another trail, and stayed pretty much on our northward course.

That night we had no shanty to sleep in. Our fire was meager, barely enough to drive the shadows back a yard or two. With no wind at all, the smoke rose in a straight plume. I thought of the Reverend Mr. Yates and his sermon about the smoke of sacrificial fire. "A pleasing odor in the nostrils of our Lord," he'd said. At the time this seemed a strange thing to preach on. But this night I fancied our little fire a kind of sacrifice. And I wondered whether God might take notice.

I prayed that Michal's illness would pass. She shook now and her eyes had a bleary, misty look to them.

The next day we saw a man on horseback. We traveled along the top of a narrow ridge. On one side the land sloped away into brush and swamp. In the other direction, the ground was barren, raw stone and gravel slides.

Michal paused and held me back. Then she looked across the vale, and there was the man. He observed us. Indeed he had seen us first. He did not signal or cry out a greeting, as one might expect in such a desolate place.

His clothes were a tattered black cloak and a broad-brimmed hat. From that distance we could not see his face. But later, Michal told me he was not one of her father's men. Still, he stared, bleak and motionless as a lightning-blasted stump.

I was about to shout a greeting, but Michal held me by the arm and whispered, "No, do not call out to him." Her grasp tightened, fear giving her uncommon strength.

"But he might tell us the way, or have a bite of food to share."

Still she forbade me. "He will not help us." And with that she led me down from the ridge's crest and the man was gone from sight.

Did he ride back toward Goodspell, I wondered. Was he even then racing to tell John Good that we had been sighted?

That night we exhausted our corn cakes and nibbled the last of the shriveled-up apples. We found a kind of rocky overhang that protected us from the wind and slept in its shelter. Tho I made a fire and gave Michal the coat which Jack Smoke had given to me, she still shook and moaned with the cold. And her tears flowed. Her weeping was like the sting of a serpent to my spirit. She depended on me as no one had ever done before. And I could give her no comfort nor even hope of comfort.

Her weeping continued, even as slumbers took her.

Not long after after setting out the next day, we rose to the crest of another ridge and got a glimpse of something bright and silvery on the horizon. "The river," I said, pointing out the far-off glimmer. "The Genesee. We'll head that way and follow it direct to Little Sion."

But my hope was not secure, for what I saw might indeed be one of the long narrow bodies of water which the Seneca called the Finger Lakes. We might in fact have been many miles too far east and could wander for days, with empty bellies.

Still, I took the flash of distant silver as a sign of hope and set off at a quicker pace.

We found a cart-track which made the going easier, and I began to feel my spirits rise. The river could not be more than a few miles away, and then surely we'd meet folks who could give us aid.

Indeed that morning we did pass by a farmstead. Now hope mounted in me just as the sun mounted the sky. We knocked at the door, but found the place abandoned. Just as folks fled the rocky fields of Connecticut to farm the wide spaces of the Genesee Valley, already people were giving up this land and moving west. In my three years at Little Sion I'd known many families who'd packed up all they had and moved out toward Ohio and Wisconsin.

This house we'd found was no hovel nor shanty. Indeed it seemed the farmer had prospered some. But, I assumed, the call of more land, better land, had drawn the family away.

However, not a mite of food remained. What they'd left had been picked over by the beasts of the woods. We might have spent the night there, warm, but the sight of the river glinting on the horizon bade me to continue.

So, hungrier for having our hopes of food raised, we set out again. "If there's a farm here, surely there will be another one nearby."

But hour after hour passed, and nothing of humanity did we see. Even the cart track dwindled to nothing, and we found ourselves again slowing.

Once, crossing a little brook, Michal stumbled and fell into the water. The rest of the day she shook, with the fever burning her as Jack Smoke had burned Goodspell.

Near dusk, I began to wonder if the sight of the river had been a vision born of hunger and the longing for home that gnawed at me with equally sharp teeth. I asked Michal if she had seen the flash of silver, but she gave no reply. Again, she was sliding into her silence and darkness. Each footstep seemed a greater effort. Each little ridge we crested was more difficult.

We trudged up yet another slope, just as the sun was dying in its crimson pall. My eyes were fixed on the ground, however, not the brilliance of the day's last light. Michal walked with her eyes closed now, her hand on my shoulder like a blind girl.

Then I heard the whicker of a horse and stopped, still as stone.

There on the ridge top stood the man we'd seen the day before. His broad-brimmed black hat was pulled low. This day, at a closer distance, I could see the features of his face. He was perhaps the age of Mr. Bonness, and the wisdom of his years was quite plain. But unlike my master, not a glint of kindness could be seen. He wore a shaggy black beard and carried a tattered black Bible in his hand.

His horse was no charger, but a bandy-legged nag. His cloak was patched and tattered. It rippled in the wind, which was now flecked with snow. Certainly his clothes, his tottering mount, his battered leathern saddle bags did not give the impression of distinction. However, his posture, stiff as a ramrod, and his expression, fierce as a winter gale, made him seem a man of great consequence. The Reverend Yates had preached on the Four Horsemen who will ride in the skies in those Final Days. Here, I thought, might be the fifth.

Tho sore afraid, hunger gave me the courage to speak.

I asked for food. He dug in one of his bags and handed me two pieces of hard cornbread. We ate these up and with no shame I asked for more. "We've had nothing in our bellies for a day and some. And my friend is very ill." He nodded and with his knife cut slices of bacon off a piece he had wrapped in oiled cloth. The meat was tough and dry as the leather of my shoes, but as it softened in my mouth, I felt the cruel pangs of hunger ebbing away.

We thanked him, and he nodded again his welcome. "Can you tell us, sir, is the river that away? Are we far?"

"A mile or two," he said. I had expected his voice to boom like the angel of death's vengeful shout. There was no fury in his tones, only a note of warning. "The river is not far ahead. But the men who search for you are not far behind."

With this, I felt an icy hand clutch at my insides. Was he one of John Good's men? Was this our end, brought to earth like foxes by this black-shrouded hunter?

"You are the two who have fled," he said. "The word travels swiftly. There is a reward for your capture. A greedy man could make a hundred dollars by galloping a few miles back and informing John Good of your presence."

Michal bowed her head, like a prisoner approaching the headsman's block. However, this man was no executioner. "There's mercy wider than any river," he said. Did he mean God's mercy, which his holy book contained? Or was he himself the merciful one? I swallowed the last of my dried bacon, more thankful for that food than for any I'd ever eaten.

The man accepted my thanks, but told me that it was my father in heaven whom I should thank. With this,

Michal winced, as tho the word *father* was a dagger in her flesh.

"You need to keep moving," the rider said, then pointed down a little dell. "Go that way, about a hundred rods and you'll find a track. Go to the west, toward the sunset. And before dark you'll come to the river."

We set off in the deepening dusk. Snow swirled above our heads like ghosts. The sunlight faded quickly, scarlet melting to shadow. The man had spoken true, for a short distance into the dell, we came to a pathway marked with fresh hoofprints.

It wasn't long before the track widened and I saw the ruts of wagon wheels. Surely a farm must be around the next bend, or the one after that. I took Michal's feverish hand to keep her moving at my pace. The river, and aid, were not far, I kept telling her. And she tried to keep up. Yes, she tried to share my hope.

But the gloom deepened. And we heard a far-off ominous sound. Michal stopped me and told me to listen. It might have been the boom of a musket, a hunter bringing down some venison for his family's nighttime meal. It came again tho, and again.

Was it a warning? Or a signal? Should we flee from

the sound, or head toward it? The black-cloaked rider had carried no firearm. Someone else was nearby.

Again Michal's tears came, and the soft sounds of weeping that seared me like a hot iron. "You go on, Albion," my friend said. "No matter how far I run, my father will find me. You keep on to the river and go back to Little Sion." I told her this was folly. I said she'd be safe at Little Sion. And then I echoed the words of the rider: "Mercy's free."

"For some," Michal said through her tears. "For some it's free and for some it will never be."

"Why should you turn back now?" I pleaded. "Why plan your escape and trek all this way and then give up?"

"Because, no matter how far I run, my father is still with me. I dream of him at night. I see him in the shadows. I close my eyes and there he is. I hear the sound of musket fire and I hear my father's voice. Locked in my room at Goodspell or fleeing to China, he's ever with me."

She sat down on the cold earth and again told me to continue. I refused, now a clench of panic grasping me. John Good was nearby, with his pack of hunters and his measureless wrath.

Again we heard the hollow boom, now closer by. I

bade her to rise and follow. I took her hand and pulled, but her resolve was iron-hard. She would stay, she said, and face her father. "I can't go on," she said. I didn't know if she meant she was overcome by illness or despair.

"Then I will stay, too," I told her. "If you insist on this, then my capture and my punishment will also be on your head." I dropped the hammer, like a mariner dropping anchor.

Through tears, she begged me to go. "No," I said. "We return to Little Sion together, or I face your father's wrath with you."

This, at last, softened her heart. She had given up hope for herself, but could not bear the thought of what her father might do to me.

So she struggled to her feet, I snatched up the hammer, and on we went, trying to keep up a quicker pace. By this time the moon was up, low and brilliant white above the trees. The path stayed largely on a straight course and the moon's brightness lit a clear way. We went over another hilltop and behind us, down in the dell where Michal had sat and refused to go on, I saw a pack of shadows moving. I was certain this was John Good and his men, but how could they be so silent?

Grasping Michal's hand, I ran. And ahead I saw a farmstead, with a light burning in one window and a plume of smoke rising from the chimney. At last, there were others. It wasn't food we needed now, however, but a tall stone wall to protect us, or an army of friends who should come to our aid. The cold air seared in and out of my lungs. How much worse was it for Michal? And my legs, already weak from our journey, were now as frail as two stalks of wheat. If I tripped on a rock, or in a hole, I should go flat to the ground and not be able to rise.

From behind us, I heard the noise of our pursuers. They'd been moving secretly, silently, but now that we'd seen them, there was no need for stealth any longer.

We ran and they ran. We rose up the ridge side, and they came down the one behind us.

Then we came to the crest, and I saw the river below us. The moon rode like a beautiful white boat on the Genesee's black water. Farther north, closer to Little Sion, the river winds and coils in on itself like a vast snake. But here it traveled smooth and straight. Willows drooped along the banks, dragging their branches in the slow-moving waters.

We paused, but only a moment.

From behind, we heard John Good's voice, a dreadful booming: "Michal! Michal!" Her reply was a feeble cough.

On the far side of the river there were crimson lights moving. Three torches, held by three dark figures, came down to the bank.

We ran on and quickly reached our side of the river.

Behind us John Good bellowed like a wounded ox. So much wrath was in his voice, but also so much wretchedness. Surely a hundred times he had fancied taking my life for stealing his daughter away from him. But perhaps there were other times when he knew that her flight was best for her.

He shouted her name again. Fury fueled that terrible sound, but loss, too.

I stepped into the cold river's water, peering at the three figures opposite. A last time John Good shouted "Michal!" and from the other side came a kind of answer. "Albion!"

I saw now that there were two men and a boy: Mr. Bonness, the Reverend Mr. Yates, and Watty. It was my young friend who called to me. "Albion!" His voice rang clear on the water, like a flute or fife. "Go up river. Just a short way, there's a raft you can ferry across in."

However, by now, John Good's pack of men had burst from the shadows. Seeing us trapped on the river's bank, they slowed their pace. John Good was at their head, a captain leading a small army of soldiers.

I was up to my knees, slipping in the icy black muck. I tugged on Michal's hand, as tho John Good were some wild animal which could not pursue us across water. But Michal would not follow me.

She shrank to the ground, head buried in her arms. Her entire body quaked, fever and fear combining to overpower her.

"Daughter," John Good said, his voice now regaining some of its lordly calm. "Daughter, rise and follow."

Again Watty shouted from the far side, and now Mr. Bonness joined his voice. "Albion!" But what good were words now? He could shout encouragement, or threats against John Good, or even prayers. But with the river between us, he might as well be a hundred miles away.

Getting no reply from Michal, John Good came to where I stood. His men hung back, as tho afraid his wrath might spill over and harm them, too. "You stole the only thing that I truly loved," he said. A cold and black calmness had replaced his fury. He might have been a deep, dry well. He might have been the burnt ruins of his house, so empty was he.

"You lied to me, you cheated me, and you stole my daughter. And even if I take her back now by the force of law or the force of arms, she is no longer mine."

I heard a splash in the water behind me, but paid it no mind, for John Good now stood like a fortress tower above me. "You have destroyed a man's only treasure." His face loomed like the moon, indeed was painted with a strange bony whiteness by the moon's cold blaze. "You came into my house like a thief and stole my precious girl from me."

The splashing grew louder, closer, and yet I heard it as if from a great distance away. John Good bore down on me, his beard quaking with the rage he tried to contain. "I should steal something from you, so that you might understand the wound you've given me. But there is nothing you have, not even your life, which you hold as dear as I held my Michal."

He lunged at her, as if to grab her away. With no thought, no idea of what I was doing, I swung the hammer with both hands. It cut a bright arc in the night air. The iron head did not touch him, but the flash of its passing did push him back.

He glared at me, his eyes throbbing with baleful light.

Tho more exhausted than I'd ever been in my life, I hefted the hammer again, cocked it back over my shoulder to strike out again if he came near Michal.

"You worm," he snarled. "You dare threaten me?"

My hands trembling, I stood like a sentinel between Michal and him.

"I should cut your flesh apart and tear out your heart, so that you can understand what you've torn away from me. My own flesh and blood! That's how dear she was to me, more precious than my own heart."

"It was her plan," I said. "It was her desire to leave."

My words stoked his rage as a strong breeze stokes the fiery coals. "What do you know of her desires?" he shouted. "How dare you presume to understand us?"

It was this which roused Michal from her silence.

She came between John Good and me, and with her weak, trembling hand easily pushed him back. "And what do you know of me?" she said. No loud bluster, but a whisper sharp as a knife blade.

He stared back at her, amazed by her defiance. At Goodspell this would have warranted the severest punishment. But here, I suppose, the rules they'd abided by were all cast to the wind.

"You don't know me," she hissed. "You have never known me. You have not the feeblest notion of who I am and what I truly want."

He drew back his hand to strike her, as a master threatens to whip his dog. But she did not flinch back. I had the hammer. I had the arms and eyes and skill to swing it true. But she moved forward, as if to protect me.

She faced him, waiting. "Do you see?" she said. "Would a man who truly knew his daughter menace her thus? Would he think he could persuade her with loud words and brute fists?"

Like a torrent of water which meets a dam and turns suddenly away, John Good's wrath veered toward me. He raged and threatened. He cursed and pointed his finger at me like a judge calling down doom on a condemned man.

Again Michal came between us. "Albion told you the truth," she said. "It was my plan and my desire. As long as I can remember, I have wanted to flee from you. So aim your rage at me, not at him. He has done nothing wrong."

John Good rose to his final height of fury, a black thunder cloud spitting out lightning. But even with his entire rabble of men behind him, he had not the strength to beat down this one sickly girl.

Then we heard a splashing sound from the river and someone clambering up the bank. "Albion is coming home," Mr. Bonness said. Another man, drenched and nearly frozen, might have seemed pathetic. But my master came to my side and made it plain that no harm should come to me.

"I did my work and I did it well," I said. "I completed the task he set for me." I wanted Mr. Bonness to know I hadn't shirked, that I wasn't a mere runaway apprentice boy. "This girl, her name is Michal, asked me for help. I fled because she —"

My master told me to shush. "You need not explain. I'm sure you've done nothing wrong."

With this John Good exploded a last time. "Nothing wrong? This whelp came into my house and covered his crimes with vile lies and then stole away my daughter as tho she were some cheap prize to be pilfered away."

"I'm certain Albion has not purposefully wronged you," my master said. "But if you think his contract unfulfilled, I'll pay you what you think fair for your losses."

"I will not haggle over dollars and pennies when a priceless treasure is being stolen before my eyes." For the first time, I saw him falter, a flicker of doubt cross his face. "Michal," he said. "Michal, look at me. How can you desert me, desert what has ever been your life? I have given you everything, all I had." His voice trailed off, like a stream of water swallowed up by dry sand.

Her whole body shook, all her sadness and pain melted like wax by her fever. She burned bright, as a candle flame given a strong draft of air. "You gave me nothing but sorrow. Nothing but grief deeper and darker than any cave."

"Go then!" John Good bellowed. "I should have seen from the first that this cur would blacken our door.

I should have seen he was as a plague carrier and once he'd crossed my threshold, all would be tainted. You are poisoned, polluted!" he screamed. "You are my daughter no longer."

"I never was your daughter. Not truly." Her voice came soft and hollow.

With that, John Good turned his back on us. Yet he did not retreat one step. Michal repeated her words, but he seemed not to hear a thing. He stood on the river bank, a statue carved of darkest stone. His men stayed back, more afraid of him than me, I suppose.

We left that place, but looking back once from a distance, I saw him still there, hard and black and unmoving.

Mr. Bonness hurried us along the river bank until we found the raft. Soon we were across and warming ourselves around a fire. Watty rejoiced to see me, to know no harm had come to me. But he regarded Michal in a curious way, unsure how best to treat her.

I explained what had happened, in a crazyquilt manner I'm sure, stitching my story together from bits and pieces. I asked how far we were from Little Sion and was overjoyed to hear we could reach the town that night.

"How did you know we were here?" I asked, after Mr. Bonness and Michal warmed enough to move on. "How did you know to come to this place?"

The Reverend Mr. Yates explained that a circuit-riding preacher had come to town the day before, and tho he was a wild and curious person, in tattered black cloak and grizzled beard, he was clearly a man of God. And he told of seeing two young people, Michal and me, of course, wandering lost. This was after seeing him the first time, from across the valley.

"But how did you know to come to that place on the river? How did you know we'd be there tonight?"

Watty said, "I was Listening Hard." Before, Mr. Bonness had no tolerance for Watty's strange ways and fanciful sayings. But tonight he did not tell him be quiet. "I listened every night you were gone, Albion. When you left I heard your footsteps in the woods and Nessie's sorry old panting. And as you got farther and farther away the sound got quieter. But I never once lost it. If I tried, if I made myself quiet and Listened Hard, if I sat by the window at night, I could hear."

We walked along the pathway in the fading moonlight. In the black surface of the river, I could see little pinpricks of stars. We were quiet a long while. Then Watty started up again. "I heard your hammer, Albion. Tap tap tap: three and then a pause. I heard it at night. And I heard voices I didn't know. And I heard the crackle of fire. And I heard a girl crying, and I suppose that must have been you," he said taking Michal's hand.

"I told Papa that a girl was crying down here on the river. And after what Mr. Yates had heard from the rider, we had to come down and find you."

We spoke more, explaining, asking questions, telling stories of the last two months. But Michal said nothing. The effort of defying her father's will had sapped the last of her strength. Her fever waxed hotter. Soon it was impossible for her to walk. Mr. Bonness and the Reverend Yates took spells carrying her back, which slowed our progress considerable.

Our talk dwindled down to nothing, and we struggled along in silence. By the time we reached Little Sion, the moon was gone and the sky was thick with stars.

It is now two months hence, and yesterday we laid Michal in her grave. Her fever broke, but then came back again fierce as a lightning storm. Mrs. Bonness took tender care of Michal, as tho she were her own natural daughter. Doctor Billings came, but no aid could save her life. She lingered, weak and barely able to speak, for a while. Then she seemed to regain her strength and called for me. We talked of where she'd go when she got well, first to Manhattan and then over the ocean. I brought her a few books with engravings of wonderful scenes. We pored over these a long while, and then Michal fell into a peaceful kind of sleep.

But her illness had merely pulled back, like a fighter who withdraws to regain his power for a final attack. And when it came again, chills and shakes and sweats awful to behold, she could no longer fend it off.

It was hard going, breaking the frozen ground with a pick axe, but down a foot or so the earth was soft enough to dig. Mr. Bonness told me he'd help with the work, but I wanted to do it all myself. Swinging the pick, stabbing with the shovel, I could pour out some of my grief. We laid her to rest beside the two Bonness girls. Tho my master and his wife had known Michal only a few weeks, they grieved for her long and true.

Mr. Bonness has found me a big piece of marble and

given leave for me to devote my time to its carving. I hope to make a fine monument for Michal. Whether the one back at Goodspell survived the fire and John Good's wrath, I do not know. But this one will stand, I hope, until God calls us all home.